A DEADLY ~~DEAL~~

Salwen was at a corner banquette that surveyed the elegant dining room. He smiled at Emily, gestured for her to join him, poured her a glass of wine. Emily sat, ignored the glass, and stared into the older man's face.

Smiling, conversational, Salwen said, "Emily, I'm offering you a bargain. One hundred percent clearance. The FBI off your case."

Emily waited.

Salwen continued, "All I want in return is a simple truth. Who knows what you know?"

How strange, Emily suddenly thought with wonder. *I have something he wants. He thinks I have something he wants.* She heard her own voice as if from far away. "I'll make a deal."

Salwen was on guard now.

"I'll tell you who knows. You—" Emily had to pause for breath. "You tell me who killed the boy."

Salwen shook his head, a teacher disappointed in a promising pupil.

Emily began to tremble . . .

"*You* killed him, Emily. He'd be alive if it wasn't for you . . ."

THE HOUSE ON CARROLL STREET

A Novel by Mollie Gregory
Based on the Screenplay by Walter Bernstein

POCKET BOOKS

New York   London   Toronto   Sydney   Tokyo

This novel is a work of fiction. Names, characters, places and incidents are either a product of the author's imagination or are used fictitiously. Any resemblance to actual events or locales or persons, living or dead, is entirely coincidental.

Another *Original* publication of POCKET BOOKS

POCKET BOOKS, a division of Simon & Schuster, Inc.
1230 Avenue of the Americas, New York, N.Y. 10020

ISBN: 0-671-64017-8

First Pocket Books printing February 1988

10 9 8 7 6 5 4 3 2 1

POCKET and colophon are trademarks of
Simon & Schuster, Inc.

Printed in the U.S.A.

—THE HOUSE ON—
CARROLL STREET

Chapter 1

On the day it all began, Emily Crane was looking at a picture of a GI in Korea.

The powerful photograph showed a M.A.S.H. nurse bending over the GI. She was fighting a spurt of blood from his neck. His leg was bandaged and bloodied; his mouth open in agony. *Sharp focus, good composition*, Emily thought, peering at it. *Extremely moving, too.* Emily wondered if the nurse had won the battle and saved the soldier's life.

Emily's office was bare and functional, but she'd covered the walls with photographs of various sizes and subjects. Some of the photographers had inscribed their pictures to Emily. She was proud of her friendships with the men and women whose pictures illustrated so much of life.

"How's the prettiest, smartest woman in my department?"

Warren Barringer stood in her office doorway. He was a tall man, about forty-five, who stooped slightly. He had curly gray hair, horn-rim glasses, and a round face with deep vertical lines in his cheeks. His manner slid between fatherly affection and mild flirtation.

"Fine. These pictures for the Korean spread are searing, Warren," Emily said, her brow knit in sincerity.

Warren took one step into her cubicle and peered over her shoulder. "Humm, lotta blood. Too shocking. What else you got?"

"This one." She showed him a GI sitting somewhere muddy and cold. He had a blanket pulled over the back of his head, a canteen cup in his hand, and he looked out of the picture with haunted, glowing eyes.

"That's it!" Warren said. "You have a real talent for spotting pictures, Em." He smiled at her.

Emily Crane was twenty-five, an up-and-coming picture editor who'd been with Barringer's department at *LOOK* magazine since 1948 when she'd graduated from Vassar. She was quite beautiful, aware of her looks but not self-conscious. She tried not to draw attention to herself. Her shoulder-length blond hair was cut in a simple pageboy, she used very little make-up, and her light hazel eyes nearly always shone with good humor. In fact, that's what Warren liked best about Emily: she worked hard and well, but she never lost her sense of humor.

"I think that one's the best, too," she said. "If it's okay with you, Warren, I want to leave a little early tonight."

"Big date?"

"Yes. Peter." She grinned.

"Ah, the famous Peter," he said, pleased for her.

"We're going to see *The King and I*."

"I haven't seen it yet but Marge is dying to go," Warren said. "I hear it's terrific!" It was the biggest hit in town. Warren lit a cigarette and inhaled deeply.

"Oh, take that thing outta here," Emily cried, waving her hand in the air. "I'm trying to give it up."

"That's great, Em. Takes willpower, but you have plenty of that."

"I haven't had a cigarette in—" She rolled her eyes skyward. A sly, pretty smile indented her cheeks. "In fifty-five hours!"

"Okay, take whatever time you need. But I'm leaving you in charge of the Korean layout."

"Oh, Warren, such power!" Emily laughed. She liked working with him.

"Just run it by me. I trust you completely—the woman who'll probably have my job in a year!" He patted her shoulder and turned to leave.

"Who'd want your job?" she called after him. She looked at the chaos on her desk. "Time for coffee," she muttered, and made her way to the little room at the end of the corridor where a coffeepot was always kept hot, and a few machines with candy bars leaned against the wall. She was pouring the coffee when Tommy came in.

"You beat me to it!" he exclaimed. "I was going to bring you some." Tom was the picture department's office boy, cheerful and ambitious.

"Why, thanks, Tommy," she said. He was

eighteen, but he looked about fifteen. He had a freckled face and a sunny manner that always reminded her of her brother, Jeff. Jeff had drowned under the ice in a Connecticut pond when he was fifteen. Emily had been the elder by a year; they'd been skating together when the ice buckled, and he'd gone in. She'd done everything she could to save him, but she had failed, and the residue of guilt still remained.

Since that terrible winter, Emily always noticed and felt protective toward boys around that age. She'd struck up a solid friendship with Tommy. She liked his looks, lean and vulnerable: the way of young boys on the edge of manhood.

"Isn't tonight *The King and I* night?" he asked, taking the cup she'd poured for him.

"Yes. Pete got orchestra seats!"

"He still with the district attorney?"

"Sure. He's a full-fledged lawyer," she said. "We've been dating, gosh, about six months now." She'd met Peter through friends on the magazine, and they'd liked each other immediately. "Gotta go," she said. "Have a whole picture essay to put together."

Her phone was ringing when she got back. "Yes?" she said into the receiver.

"There's a man out here asking for you," said the receptionist.

"Who?" asked Emily.

"Didn't say."

Emily hung up and bounced out of her office into the long corridor that was lined with cubicle offices just like hers. As she passed the open doors she could hear snatches of conversation, the buzz and hum of the weekly magazine that most of America read. She pushed open the door to the reception area.

"Okay, I'm here," she said to the receptionist who had just started working for *LOOK*.

A pale man in dark wrinkled clothes approached her. He was about fifty and had a humble yet truculent air that put her off. "Miss Crane?" he asked.

"Yes."

"Assistant picture editor?"

"Yes."

Smirking, he furtively slipped a folded piece of paper out of his jacket.

"What's that?" asked Emily.

"A subpoena," he said. "From the Congress of the United States." He turned on his heel, his job done, and cried "Hold it!" to the elevator's closing doors.

"Wait!" cried Emily. But the man was gone. She stared at the piece of paper, folded and thick. It looked terribly official.

"Marilyn," Emily said. She was back in her office and on the telephone. Marilyn had been her college roommate and was her best friend in New York. Emily gripped the telephone and tried to keep her hand from shaking. "Does this mean what I think it means?"

Marilyn sounded tired and harried. "Yes, Emily, it does. So far three of us have a subpeona. We're going to have an emergency meeting this afternoon at five o'clock. You'll be there?"

"Yes," Emily murmured, thinking of the other people in the organization she'd joined. It was called Liberty Watch. She wrestled with her growing sense of depression. "Don't let anyone in the door unless they have their subpoena," she joked, but Marilyn didn't laugh.

She reached Peter by telephone as he was leaving his office. Quietly, she told him what happened.

"You were *what*?" he cried in disbelief. She could hear him kicking the door of his office closed.

"Subpoened."

"My God, it must be some ghastly mistake," he said. He had an articulate, brittle way of speaking. She could picture him, lean and lanky, wearing a suit and tie, handsomely conservative, perched on the corner of his desk. He always seemed to be temporarily seated as if he might take flight at any moment.

"It isn't a mistake, Pete," she said, feeling as if she had to convince him of her innocence. "They're after the Liberty Watch group, and I'm a member. I just talked to Marilyn—"

"She's married to the lawyer?"

"Yes. But I was calling you—"

"But you're not a communist," he said combatively.

"Of course not, but—"

"Why are you mixed up with that group, anyway?"

"Peter!" Emily stared at the pictures covering her desk. Speaking to Peter was not turning out to be the comfort she'd imagined. "I'm calling you because I can't have dinner. I'll have to meet you at the theater. We're having an emergency meeting—"

"Don't go near those people, Emily!"

"I'm sorry, Peter, I've got to go. There's a lot of strategy—"

"You'll only make it worse!" He clapped his hand over the receiver and yelled at someone. "I wish I'd known you were mixed up—"

"Peter, I've got to go. I'll see you at seven-forty-five." She hung up feeling hollow and lonely. Over the months, Peter had become important to her—his sharp wit and his instant grasp of so many different issues delighted her. He was always good company. But more than that, just last month, they had begun "to get serious," as her mother called it.

Emily glanced down at her desk. The photo of the GI in Korea stared back at her. "You and me both, fella," she said. "Tough times."

The early fifties in New York resonated with songs like "Hello Young Lovers," "Come On-a My House" and "Shrimp Boats." In the six years since the end of the war, soldiers had digested their experiences in war and translated them into big novels: *From Here to Eternity*, *The Caine Mutiny*, and *The Cruel Sea*.

Marlon Brando was the biggest new star in America, having translated his stage role of Stanley Kowalski into the movie of *Streetcar*

Named Desire. The African Queen had just opened, and so had *American in Paris*. The lines to see them formed around the block at the big Broadway theaters. Rough teenagers had adopted the greaser look—duck tails, and black leather jackets; they rolled a pack of cigarettes up in the short sleeves of their T-shirts. Middle-class teenage boys wore flat-top haircuts like the Kingston Trio; their girls went around in penny loafers or saddle shoes and reversed their cardigan sweaters, wearing the buttons down the back.

Though World War II had made America the most powerful nation in the world, a new threat to the nation's security had emerged and it was noisily blowing across the nation: communism. A wave of congressional hearings had been launched to investigate communist infiltration in government and in American life. A sort of mass hysteria seized the country: There were demands that books be taken off the library shelves; there were howls that schools and movies were communist oriented, that teachers should be screened and films censored.

Russia had recently signed a treaty with Red China, and just geographically, the size of that alliance shocked the West. Employers were demanding loyalty oaths from all personnel; those who refused to sign were dismissed. Many people stuck to their principles, pointing out that the Constitution guaranteed Americans freedom of beliefs, speech, and press. A national debate raged with the lines between contestants firmly drawn. The Rosenbergs had been tried and found guilty of treason, and they'd just been sentenced to death. The atom bomb—droppped for the first time on Hiroshima in 1945, and tested on far away Pacific islands since then—had shown that miles of life could vanish in seconds.

The early fifties were a dangerous time of deep currents and tricky shoals. Some steering mechanism had broken down, some impulse had decayed. America curled in upon itself, peeking out of backyard bunkers, built in case Russia dropped the bomb on America. By comparison, the thirties and forties seemed simpler, more understandable times. Security as it had once been known had gone forever.

The *LOOK* magazine building was in New York City's midtown area, just east of Fifth Avenue. Marilyn and Alan Dworkin, Emily's friends, were in the West Seventies. When Emily emerged from work, the late afternoon had a snappy springlike air. She decided to walk. There were few cities in the world as easy to walk in as New York. But besides that, walking helped sort out her thoughts. The subpoena and Peter's angry reaction had shaken her. They had talked a lot of politics but Peter had seemed to enjoy the friendly combat. She was sure they had discussed her work with the Liberty Watch Association, an organization that helped make connections among people working on civil liberties.

Emily Crane walked through the densely

crowded streets and thought of her job. She loved going to work each day. She was vibrantly interested in current events—which the magazine brought to her desk by the bushel. She had voted for the first time in 1948, and she'd voted for Harry Truman. Sometimes she thought she was the only person in New York who'd believed he would be elected president.

But her mother wanted her to quit her job and get married. Marriage was security. Mrs. Crane's husband had died in the thirties when Emily and her brother Jeff were children. She had raised them alone, supporting them by teaching in a grade school. It had not been easy. Emily and Jeff had spent many afternoons of their early childhood with Edna, a baby-sitter who had been with them since they were small. She'd watched over them when they got back from school for the hour or so before their mother got home.

And then Jeff had died. Mrs. Crane had gone on teaching, but she was cross and often morose. Emily had never felt as close to her mother as she had felt toward Jeff. Emily's was an optimistic, buoyant nature; Mrs. Crane always saw the downside of any situation. Emily was good in the visual arts, in music and history; Mrs. Crane taught arithmetic and science to her grade-schoolers. Emily had been delighted and relieved when she'd won a scholarship to Vassar College: it got her away from home. She knew her mother wanted her to have a better life, but of course they disagreed on how that was to be obtained. For Mrs. Crane, "a better life" could be had by marrying Peter at the first opportunity; for Emily, it was working at what she loved, and perhaps marrying later. By 1951, Emily and her mother had silently agreed to maintain the bond of mother and daughter, but it was a shell with little affection left at the center.

A high wind blew sharply off the Hudson River, skating past the brownstones that lined West Seventy-fourth Street. People scurried before it as if pushed, heading home, carrying briefcases or shouldering last-minute grocery purchases in paper sacks.

A panel truck was parked across the street from the row of brownstones. The sign painted on the side read THE AMERICAN PLUMBING SUPPLY. Inside, there were no coils or mallets or pipes or fixtures. Instead the truck was jammed with sophisticated surveillance equipment— cameras, tape recorders, sound monitors, and switches. The gear surrounded two men and gave them no comfortable spot to sit down. The younger man, Mike Cochran, focused a camera lens through a small, neatly disguised opening in the side of the truck.

"Here he comes," said the second man, Sid Hackett.

Mike Cochran's camera lens found and fixed on a middle-aged man who was going up the stairs to one of the brownstones. "Got him." The camera clicked.

"Ralph Metzger," said Hackett. "Teaches history at Columbia University. A board member of the Liberty Watch. Married with two kids."

The door to the brownstone opened, and Metzger went inside.

Cochran, at the camera, leaned back and rubbed his neck. The space was confining for a man of his size—he was over six feet—and the work was boring. Cochran was a good-looking man in his early thirties. In his youth, he'd been a natural athlete; he still loved to play baseball, but that was hard to do in New York City. He was from Kansas, and he'd been with the FBI less than three years.

"Anyway," Cochran continued. He was in the midst of describing an incident at a nearby deli. "She didn't even say thank you! I could've pocketed the dollar extra in change that she'd given me, but I didn't!" He shook his head. "She just looked at me like I was trying to put one over on her!" Cochran was by nature easygoing, but he had a midwesterner's suspicion of New York and everyone in it.

"Yup," drawled Hackett, "welcome to New York." Hackett was in his forties, and he'd been in the department for almost twenty years. He was a family man with two teenage children. His attitude toward Mike, since they'd started working on the Liberty Watch job, bordered on the fatherly. "Hey, here's another," he said as a taxi pulled up in front of the brownstone.

Cochran peered through his lens and snapped a photo of a man who was taking the stairs of the brownstone two at a time. Hackett was checking his notebooks. "That's Randolph Slote, a businessman and chairman of the Liberty Watch. He gives a lot of time and money to these causes." He chuckled, a low secret sound. "The pinker the better."

The door opened and Slote disappeared inside.

Hackett leaned back and rubbed his hands together. "You call this spring?" he demanded of his partner. "I'm freezing to death."

"Doesn't feel cold to me," said Cochran.

"That's because where you come from, twenty below is a heat wave," Hackett said.

"At least where I come from, the people aren't colder than the weather," said Mike. "It's a dry cold in Kansas, not like here. You don't feel it the same."

"Until your nose drops off." Hackett laughed as he crawled through the wires to the front of the van and turned on the engine.

"That'll look suspicious," warned Cochran, "the motor running and the truck not going anywhere." He glanced back through his camera. "Here's another, I think." He smiled. She wore a polo coat open despite the weather, a tweed skirt, and loafers. She breezed along the street, chin up, confident and pretty, like a piece of music.

"Emily Crane," said Hackett. "Assistant picture editor and a board member of their pinko organization. Hey! Take it easy with that film. We got to account to the Bureau for it."

Cochran was clicking off shot after shot. "I'm practicing my technique," he said. The girl's quick and graceful movements as she dashed up the steps and rang the bell gave him the sense that she was wonderfully alive. He just felt like taking extra frames of her.

"Then try aiming at the face, not the legs," said Hackett.

Mike pursed his lips. "I don't get it. What's a lovely girl like her doing with a bunch of Reds?"

"Sex," said Hackett, sounding avuncular. "It's all sex."

Cochran snapped Emily's picture again. A kitten that looked like a refugee crawled out of somewhere and started winding between the girl's shapely legs. She petted it, then picked it up. The door opened, but Emily didn't go inside. She was talking to another woman and showing her the cat. The woman was shaking her head. Emily Crane wasn't going to take no for an answer. "Go for it," murmured Cochran, who liked cats—they were independent.

"What?" asked Hackett.

"The girl found a kitten and wants to take it inside," he muttered, still watching. At last the other woman shrugged at Emily. "You're licked," Cochran said, smiling. "Give in." The woman held the door open and Emily and her new cat swept inside. "Ha!" snapped Cochran.

Inside, Marilyn Dworkin tried to smile at Emily but ended up looking cross. "I hope you're taking that thing home," she said.

"I am. Maybe I'll call her Liberty or Committee or First Amendment."

20

"Or Bill of Rights," muttered Marilyn. The kitten looked pathetic. "I'll bet she has fleas." She looked at Emily. "Why do you always run around with your coat open and no hat?" Marilyn was a beautiful woman, tall and willowy. She wore her long dark hair in a circular bun on the back on her head with curly little bangs in front. Marilyn had a sharp tongue in normal times; when she was anxious, it was barbed.

Emily gave her friend a quick kiss. Why shouldn't Marilyn be upset? The sky was falling. She opened her bag and drew out her subpoena. "My invitation to this party," Emily quipped. Marilyn nodded, biting the inside of her lip.

Alan came into the hall. He had a sharp attractive face with expressive eyes. He gave her a hug. "You got yours," he said. "That makes the whole board." He took the subpoena from her and scanned it.

As they started into the living room, Emily said to Marilyn, "I think Committee or Liberty needs something to eat."

"There's a platter of cheese on the coffee table," Marilyn said, sarcastically.

"How about some milk? And a cigarette?"

"I thought you stopped."

"I always drink milk," said Emily, smiling broadly.

"Smoking, chum, smoking."

"I did give it up, for sixty-two whole hours."

The Dworkins' living room was light and airy with high ceilings painted white. But the knot of ten people standing in its center could have been in a tunnel for all they noticed. They nodded tightly at Emily as she entered, but their murmured conversations went on. There was an air of controlled tension in the room. Emily took the cigarette Marilyn offered, lit it, and inhaled. She closed her eyes in sweet pleasure.

"It's almost worth being subpoened," she said, taking another drag on the cigarette. She put the kitten down.

"You're pretty cheerful about all this," said Ralph Metzger, taking notice of Emily for the first time since she'd come inside. He had a college professor's control of the room. He was fifty, and under his thick eyebrows, his sharp, pale eyes looked critical and defensive at the same time.

"You should have seen her at an eight o'clock medieval lit. class," said Marilyn, referring to their college years. "It was revolting. This is the one person I know who never goes under." She glanced at her friend. "Look at her—she's about to lose her job and she rescues a cat."

"I don't think I'm going to lose my job," Emily said. "I don't have any real power at the magazine, and Warren is protective. He'll go to bat for me." Once the thought had been expressed, Emily found herself feeling more doubtful than she sounded. But it was important to her to keep up a confident and cheerful front. She would not give in to fantasies and anxieties.

Sally Hawkins—a woman in her forties who was vice-president of the organization—came up to them. Her graying hair was fashioned in tight curls—the new poodle cut. It set off her face attractively. "Jail is not a laughing matter, Emily," she said sternly.

"When I was a kid," said Randolph Slote, "I thought I'd go to jail for stealing hubcaps. Now, it could be for contempt of Congress." Randy Slote was a lean man who never seemed to stop moving. "What I can't figure out is," he said, pretending to scowl in deep thought, "is *that* a step up or a step down?" Emily liked Randy's wry sense of humor. It often matched her mood precisely.

"No one's in jail yet," said Alan, all business. "This is only a Senate committee investigating subversive activities."

"Which means anything they want it to mean," said Metzger, the pessimist in the crowd. "They crucified those guys from Hollywood. They lost all their appeals and they're going to jail."

"For what?" asked Slote's brother, a big-boned man with a generous smile.

"For contempt of Congress," Metzger said. "They wouldn't answer the committee's question."

"Oh," he said, ironically, "the 'are you now or have you ever been a communist?'" He rattled it off like a machine gun—a rapid, staccato barrage. Metzger nodded stiffly. Marilyn reappeared with a saucer of milk for the kitten.

"Oh, for God's sake, Marilyn," said Metzger, seeing her put down the saucer of milk.

"But it's no more illegal being a communist than being a Republican," Slote said, ignoring Metzger and the saucer.

Ralph Metzger had a tendency to monopolize discussion. "We just have to be clear on what we're going to do," Alan said, taking the room back from Metzger. "The first thing the committee's going to want are our membership records and our correspondence—"

"So they can use us to reach other organizations and taint them," said Metzger.

"Right," Alan agreed, mildly irritated. He was fond of Metzger and understood his need to be center stage. "We need to decide who hangs on to the list."

Emily had drifted over to the window and stared out at Seventy-fourth Street, enjoying her cigarette.

"This includes you, Emily," Alan said, irritated.

"I have nothing to hide. I'll talk to the committee," she said without turning around.

"What?" cried Metzger, appalled. He turned to the group for confirmation. "We can't testify! We're citizens! No one—not even Congress—has the right to ask *citizens* what they believe in. There's a principle here, Emily!"

"We shouldn't say anything!" cried Slote's brother.

Sally chimed in: "We should take the Fifth! The committee's unconstitutional and everyone knows it! If we answer we're just condoning what they're doing. It's a witch hunt!"

"Let's define some areas here." Marilyn

moved in to prevent Metzger from giving a lecture. Marilyn understood Emily a great deal better than they did. Emily's confident, agile air covered a deeply serious part of her character that many people misunderstood.

But Emily needed no protection. She faced the friends with whom she'd worked for so long. "You all know me. I said I'd *talk* to the committee, but if they want me to sign a loyalty oath or betray this organization, I won't do it," she said. "I am the secretary of Liberty Watch, I've got the lists, and I'll protect them." She stabbed out her cigarette reluctantly. "We have our rights. We're not traitors. We haven't broken any laws. We should keep those things in mind."

Alan sighed loudly. "Emily, they don't care about that."

"They may not, but I do," Emily responded quickly.

"And they won't stop with subpoenas," Alan went on. "They'll try to scare you and intimidate you. Take a look out there," he said, striding to the window. "You see that truck with the motor running? That's the FBI. They're taking pictures of everybody who comes into this house."

Emily had noticed the truck as she stood at the window. Now she shook her head in a kind of wonder. What kind of creeps would do such things, spy on other people? But at the back of her bravado and her truly sunny nature, she felt that a net was being drawn around her by unseen hands. She picked up the kitten and ran a finger along its bony back.

* * *

The cemetery in Queens was empty except for one lone burial. The rabbi read over a coffin as a pair of gravediggers lowered it into the open grave. No mourners crowded around in the cold, gray light; no one wept for the loss of the man who had entered, endured, and departed his life, and no children clung to the skirts of the widow.

As the rabbi finished reading, the gravediggers hastily and unceremoniously started shoveling dirt over the coffin. The only sound other than the scrape of their spades was the low murmur of the wind.

Unseen, a thin boy of sixteen peeped out from behind a tombstone where he'd been hiding. He was waiting for the lonely ritual to finish. Around him, in the gathering darkness, an acre of gravestones resembled a silent, miniature city of skyscrapers. He shivered from the chill, but cold was nothing new to Stefan Hudak. He had outlasted much worse. He pinched his eyes shut and put one hand inside his pocket. The other moved to his mouth in an unconscious gesture, a bent thumb pressed to his lips, curiously childlike. The wind lifted his light brown hair from the back of his head. He opened his eyes and, hunched against the wind, waited patiently until the rabbi walked off. The two men tramped down the earth on the grave, then hustled off with their shovels.

After a moment, Stefan looked around in all directions. When he was satisfied that he was alone, he crept to the grave and peered near-sightedly at the tombstone. It read MEYER TE-PERSON 1898–1951. He took a pad and pencil from his pocket and, forcing his cold fingers to work, wrote down the name from the tomb-stone.

Chapter 2

One of Emily's first memories was standing in the Lincoln Memorial below the enormous statue of the president, looking up at his huge bronze knee. It had been spring, and the smell of the cherry blossoms had wafted into the open monument. Her father had held one of her hands, and she had held her brother's hand, she remembered, and her father had said in his soft voice, "Abe Lincoln was a man of peace, a common man who rose to do uncommon things for his country."

Since that time, Emily had revisited Washington, D.C., the city-center heart of the nation, walking the wide streets and touring the marble buildings—the architectural symbols of the freest, finest government on earth.

But now, in a Senate hearing room, she was terrified. She was sitting at a table facing five senators on a dais in front of her. Alan Dworkin was beside her. Behind them, the small hearing room was crammed with unruly spectators. All around her there was a sense of disorder and confusion, as though some central fixative of life had worn out. A section of spectators' seats was reserved for the press, and against the wall four cameramen from the newsreels had set up their equipment. Behind the senators, another crowd of people—assistants, counsels, and investigators—ceaselessly came and went, adding to the barely controlled frenzy in the room. Between the witness table, where Emily sat, and the dais, the court stenographers held a calm, neutral middle ground.

"It's like a public execution," Emily whispered to Alan.

Startled, he stared at her. He thought it a dreadful thing for a young woman to say. "Quite overstated, Emily," he said, rebuking her.

To calm the birds that had taken flight in the pit of her stomach, Emily concentrated on her accusers—the investigating senators on the dais.

Senator Byington, about forty, was the best-looking man up there, and the most liberal—which was a little like saying that a Republican from Oregon might be a little more liberal than a Democrat from Arkansas. He had black wavy hair, large, tolerant, and at times bemused eyes, and a generous mouth. The other senators looked like lumpen politicos without definable character.

But next to Byington sat the chief committee counsel, Samuel Salwen. Since Emily had been brought in the room, Salwen had been scribbling notes. He had a long face, thick sandy hair, a high forehead, and sharp dark eyes that didn't miss much. He was constantly signaling people to approach him. He'd whisper in the ear of whoever came up to him, and then wave them away with a smile, a warm handshake, or a nod. Samuel Salwen had a lot of power.

"Where's he come from?" Emily asked Alan, nodding at Salwen.

"Salwen? From a very old and distinguished upper New York State family. Revolutionary colonels, Continental Congress, and railroad magnates. Or maybe just land, I forget. He's the most eligible bachelor in town." Alan winked at her, trying to put her at ease.

Emily watched Salwen, fascinated by his confident manner and his energy, which he held in check with a slight air of boredom. *It's almost as though too much energy or excitement is in bad taste*, she thought.

Senator Byington chaired the committee. He banged the gavel down smartly and called for order. Emily was the third witness that morning. The noise abated a little, but the cameras started to whirr. Flashbulbs popped like tiny explosions in front of her face and the chairman's.

Emily's mouth went dry as she heard Byington say: "Miss Emily Crane?"

"Yes," she said, nodding nervously.

"What is your full name, please?"

"Emily Elizabeth Crane."

"Where do you reside?" Senator Byington asked. He had a deep, rich voice.

"New York City," she said. Her throat was not cooperating and it was hard to get a breath.

"Would you mind speaking into the microphone?" asked Senator Newton from Illinois. He was an elderly man with a tight mouth and red cheeks. Emily wondered if he was one of the senators who wore makeup for the newsreel cameras.

Emily moved closer to the microphone and in doing so discovered that her body was as rigid as a board. "New York City," she repeated breathily. Her warm, ripe voice had vanished.

"Where are you employed?" asked Byington.

"I'm an assistant picture editor at *LOOK* magazine," she said with a little more confidence.

"Miss Crane," Salwen said into his mike, not looking up, "are you a member of the board of an organization called Liberty Watch?" His voice matched his looks—elegant, slightly contemptuous, intelligent.

"Yes, I am a member," Emily said. "You already know that." She astonished herself. Suddenly she wasn't afraid of them.

"This is for the *record*, Miss Crane," said Salwen, still not looking at her. "Now, if we could get on, does the subpoena you received direct you to bring with you here all books, ledgers, records, and papers relating to that organization?"

"Yes, it does," she said clearly. She'd found her voice.

"And did you bring them?"

"I have a statement here I'd like to read," she said.

"Oh, Miss Crane," Salwen said, looking up for the first time. "Please answer the question." He smiled. It was later that she realized his smile was one of anticipation.

"I think my statement will—"

"We will consider your statement in due time, Miss Crane," Byington said, in a reasonable voice without a trace of sarcasm.

"We are an organization devoted to the cause of civil liberties," Emily began, but Salwen cut her off.

"We know all about your organization, Miss Crane. That's why you're here."

But Emily was not to be deterred. "We make no political conditions. We—"

"Do you deny this committee—"

"In our files," Emily said firmly, looking up at him, "are the names of people we have helped and people who have helped us. I won't be part of getting them in trouble. Just because—"

Salwen smiled again, more broadly, and put down his pen. "A great publication, *LOOK* magazine. Don't you agree?"

"Yes," she said guardedly.

"A circulation of millions," Salwen went on, looking up at the high-vaulted ceiling. "Each week, *LOOK* gives us a picture view of the world's events. And you select those pictures, Miss Crane." His gaze drifted down from the ceiling to rest on her. "I'm impressed."

"I don't decide what goes into the magazine," she said.

"But you have the power to suggest!" he cried, pouncing on her.

"Mr. Chairman—" began Alan.

But Senator Byington anticipated his protest.

"Mr. Salwen," Byington said, "I don't see how any of this relates."

Salwen held up a sheaf of papers and waved them dramatically. "Ah, but it does," Salwen said to the senator. He turned back to Emily. "You recognize these petitions, Miss Crane? The Stockholm Peace Petition, the World Disarmament—"

Alan jumped in. "Mr. Chairman, I object!"

But Salwen, oblivious, kept on going. "Ban the Bomb and many more of the same. *Your* signature is on all of them." He lowered his voice. "You write a lovely hand." The audience had caught on to Salwen as one of the great actors in congressional drama. He played with witnesses until they submitted to him, and then he moved on to other meals. "These *are* your signatures?"

"Yes, but it's—"

"Mr. Chairman," said Alan, exasperated, "none of this is relevant!"

"You brought these petitions to your office, didn't you?" Salwen's silky voice demanded of Emily; he ignored Alan. "You got others to sign them, didn't you?"

"Mr. Chairman!" roared Alan, rising out of his chair.

"Did they know what they were signing, Miss Crane?" Salwen hammered relentlessly. "Or were they just dupes?"

Byington rapped his gavel halfheartedly.

Emily cried, "I never lied to anyone!"

Salwen, Alan, and Emily all began talking at once but Salwen's powerful voice overrode those at the witness table. "Was it easy, Miss Crane?" he bellowed, narrowing his eyes. "How did you persuade them? A beautiful young woman such as yourself—"

Alan was furious. "I object to this line of questioning! It's absolutely—"

"May we guess at your powers of persuasion?" Salwen demanded of Emily, paying no attention to Alan.

"Mr. Salwen," said Byington firmly, banging his gavel now. "I do think—"

Salwen glanced at him. "Mr. Chairman, the witness is in a position to distort information received by millions of unsuspecting Americans."

"That's ridiculous!" cried Emily angrily.

Salwen continued like a steamroller. "Furthermore," he went on, "she has refused to turn over her files to this committee as ordered in her subpoena."

Byington was still trying to be fair. "Miss Crane, you know we have a legal right to those records."

But Emily was still furiously focused on Salwen. "But I know what you want them for," she said. "To smear people."

"Then you deny this committee—" Salwen said.

"I will *not* give you their names," Emily shouted. "And I am *not* convinced that the committee has a legal right in face of the Constitution's First, Fourth—"

"We're wasting time," Salwen said in a tired voice. "I believe a citation is called for." He went back to his papers, as though bored with the whole proceeding.

"—and the Fifth Amendments!" Emily finished triumphantly.

"I don't want to do this, Miss Crane," said Byington, "but you don't leave us much choice."

"Move the question," said Senator Newton, pursing his ruby lips and shuffling some papers impatiently.

"The law is very clear," Byington said reluctantly. "You're sure you won't reconsider?"

"I will not. Cooperation with the committee on such matters is cooperation with the dismantling of our freedoms." As she stopped to take a breath, Alan put a restraining hand on her arm.

Byington shook his head regretfully. "I'm truly sorry to hear you say that," he said to her. Then, in a more formal voice, he went on. "I move we cite this witness as being in contempt of the Congress and take steps to bring this to the floor of the Senate. All in favor."

All the senators except Byington raised their hands.

Senator Newton said pointedly, "I move we make this unanimous." Byington raised his hand. "Motion carried." He rapped his gavel. "This hearing is adjourned for lunch." Byington stood up as the other senators started conferring with their staffs and each other. A lone photographer rushed up, snapped Emily's picture, then darted away. The cameras stopped whirring. The volume in the room shot up. Everyone was standing or talking or rushing out of the hearing room.

It was over and Emily felt as forgotten as yesterday's pamphlet. "Guess that's that," she shouted in Alan's ear.

He squeezed her arm. "You were great, very courageous," he said.

"It's kinda like the French Revolution, isn't it?" she said, watching all the senators milling about, talking to each other. "Only we don't lose our heads."

At that moment Salwen clapped his hands loudly and everyone broke away from their conversations to stare at him. He motioned to the rear of the room. The doors opened and two children came trotting through them followed by an attractive woman in her midthirties. The children were solemnly carrying a birthday cake with lighted candles. As they moved toward an astonished Byington, Salwen started to sing: "Happy birthday to you, happy birthday to you . . ." The children and the women and some of the senatorial staff started to join in threadily, "Happy birthday, dear Senator . . ." The children reached the dais and Salwen gave them a hand, placing the cake in front of Byington.

Astonished, Emily watched the happy family scene. The other senators and the staffs crowded around, congratulating Byington. His children hugged him and his wife kissed him. Beaming, Salwen was at the center of it all, a proprietary arm around Byington. They seemed connected in some deeper way than as a counsel to his chief.

"Let's get out of here," Alan said, frowning.

"Yeah, I want some fresh air," said Emily. Laughter and birthday cheer followed them out. At the door, she turned. Salwen was bending toward Byington and whispering in his ear as Byington began to cut the cake.

About a week later Tommy, the picture department's office boy, was swinging down the corridor on his rounds delivering interoffice mail. He opened doors into small offices and tossed in envelopes or handed them to whoever was there.

"Pay day!" he called out with a smile as he dropped an envelope on Emily's desk. His smile faded. "Gee, you look glum."

"Oh, no," she said, brightening. "It's okay."

Her blond hair gleamed under the light, but her eyes looked sad and lonely. "Fight with Pete?" he asked.

She nodded. It was easier to nod than to explain everything. She hadn't told anyone at the magazine about her summons to Congress, and fortunately there had been no publicity that she'd seen of her appearance before the committee. But these things did not remain secret long, and she was waiting for the shoe to drop. She was sure that when it became common knowledge at *LOOK*, Tom would be one of the first to know.

"Well!" he said with the slightly self-conscious confidence of the young, "Chin up. All lovers quarrel."

"Right," she said, and waved her pay envelope at him. "Thanks, Tommy."

She put the envelope aside and finished going over a sheet of contact prints, marking the ones she liked with a red crayon.

The photos were of the marines' assault on Seoul in Korea. The city was in ruins from the bombardment of mortars. Its destruction depressed Emily; it paralleled her affair with Peter, also in ruins. They had met at *The King and I,* but had quarreled that night about her subpoena. He had wanted her to quit Liberty Watch; she had refused. His hands had chopped the air, and he looked at her as if he hated her. But they patched it up, and met for lunch later in the week. Again, he had demanded that she stay out of politics—it was degrading, messy, dangerous. Again she had refused, aghast at the violence of his feelings. "No wife of mine is ever to have anything to do with politics!" he shouted.

She had telephoned him later that day, but he had not returned the call. She telephoned again and again. When she reached him, his message had been chilly and final: "We don't believe in the same things, Emily. Don't call me again." And he hung up. Marilyn had said it was surgical, so typical of a lawyer in the district attorney's office. But Emily missed the Peter she had known before her subpoena and her political beliefs had come between them.

She put the depressing Korea photos away and took out a contact sheet of fashion photos to cheer herself up. She loved clothes and bought magazines—*Vogue, Harper's Bazaar*—every month. Dresses were really changing, much more form-fitting. The hems were going way down to the middle of the calf. The Dior stuff looked sleek. Hats were still in, she saw happily, but they were bigger. She stopped on one that looked like a flying saucer—as flat as a disk with a feather curling around the brim.

When she finished the sheet, she felt better. She opened her pay envelope idly and took out the check. "Oh, my God," she said, staring at it, stunned. She felt a chill run up her spine like a shiver, only deeper.

She pushed her chair back and strode down the narrow corridor to Warren's office. Warren was proud of his corner office and often stood at the window looking down on the street fifteen floors below. Emily avoided the window. She was afraid of heights and suffered from vertigo. Once she had almost fainted watching a parade from this very window.

Warren sat behind his substantial desk with a stack of papers in front of him. Framed prize-winning, autographed photos resided proudly on a shelf behind him and on a small antique table by the leather sofa.

Emily marched up to his desk and handed him her check. "That's four times what I make, Warren," she said.

Warren grimaced, looked at the check, then stared at the corner of his desk. "Think of it as a, well, a bonus," he said quietly. He looked embarrassed and shifted in his chair.

"But this is not a bonus, is it?" she said evenly, fixing his eyes with her own.

He glanced to his left. "You weren't supposed

to get that before you were told," he said with
genuine regret. The meeting he'd had with his
own boss a couple of days ago still made him
cringe. He'd wanted to protect her, but Bert had
been adamant. Anyone who didn't answer the
committee's questions—practically anyone who
even appeared before the committee—was out.

"Tell me now, Warren," she said. "You're the
guy who hired me. Are you firing me?"

"It wasn't my decision," he said quickly, fer-
vently. He started moving papers around on his
desk, frantically trying to think of something
she'd believe that would soften the blow. Times
were so hard now; one word whispered about
anyone, and that person was out. The only way
anyone was safe was to keep quiet and duck.
"We're reorganizing the department. Cutting
down." Emily made no move and no comment.
"Retrenching," he said with more energy. She
just looked at him. She wasn't buying it. "You
know how they get upstairs," he said miserably,
trying to dust off the responsibility. He felt like a
heel, but what was a guy to do, he asked himself.
If he hadn't agreed to fire her—if he'd stuck up
for her—they would have fired him, too. He just
couldn't afford to risk his job. Better Emily than
himself, he'd just about convinced himself before she walked in.

She stared at him. "Warren, we've always
been straight with each other—"

"It's not you!" he said quickly. "Everyone likes
you. You've got a great eye for a news picture.
It's—business. They can't afford to offend public
opinion."

"They *make* public opinion," she said.

The way she remained standing there was making him intensely uncomfortable. This slip of a girl had found the guts to defy Congress. It made him look like a coward. And he turned that bad feeling toward her now, as outright anger.

"Why the hell couldn't you cooperate?" he demanded. "Your goddamned testimony, what's the big deal? Don't you know what's going on, the climate and all? You had a future here!"

"Thanks for the truth," she said quietly.

"You quote me and I'll deny it," he warned her.

She nodded, sadly, and turned to go. He got up from his desk and put his arm around her. "Hell, Emily, I'm sorry. But you'll be fine. You've got friends, you'll find another job. Just remember—I'm in your corner." He smiled tightly.

Emily glanced up at him. Warren didn't look like he was in anyone's corner but his own.

In Washington, D.C., Samuel Salwen, Ralph Metzger, and his attorney, Harvey Griffin, were locked in battle in Salwen's office. As the committee's counsel, Salwen interviewed all witnesses scheduled to testify in a private meeting before they appeared in open session. Sometimes he got valuable information in these closed meetings.

"I can't do that," whined Metzger, sweating. He looked wildly around the room for help.

"I can be much tougher in public," Salwen said to Metzger, who was staring at a model of a frigate on Salwen's desk. "Why don't you do yourself a favor and come clean?" Metzger shook his head. "No?" Salwen asked sweetly. "Then I'll break you!" he shouted. He was enjoying himself.

"Mr. Salwen!" Griffin interrupted. "My client came here—"

"He came here to make a deal!" snarled Salwen. "He wants protection! But he can't have it unless he cooperates!" Salwen whirled on Metzger. "You were saying about your organization's membership and contacts?"

Metzger was cornered and desperate. He saw his life, job, and reputation disintegrating. "I can't stand it, Harv. I can't get up there in public. I don't have tenure at the university. I'm going to—"

"Ralph, wait." Griffin pulled Metzger aside to confer, but his client was adamant: he couldn't take the pressure. He had to find a way out.

Quietly, Metzger named the organizations that he remembered from the Liberty Watch list. "I need proof, Mr. Metzger! Not just your say-so," demanded Salwen.

"Emily Crane has all the lists!" cried Metzger, broken and hating himself.

Chapter 3

"Well, dear, of course I think you're very brave, but you were always so headstrong," Emily's mother said, cocking an eye at her. They were having dessert at Schrafft's. Her mother was wearing her "Manhattan" outfit: modest gray suit, ruffled white blouse, a tiny pillbox hat with a veil. "But I know you'll land on your feet," Mrs. Crane went on. "You always do. Whatever happened to that nice young man?"

"Peter." Emily sighed. "Peter didn't want to be too close to a 'communist.'"

"Oh, nonsense, dear. You're not a communist!"

"Of course not, Mother. But anyone who's called in front of Congress is assumed to be a 'Red.'" It was always so difficult talking to her mother.

"Why, they are not, Emily," Mrs. Crane said. She was uninterested in politics, had signed her loyalty oath to remain on as a teacher, and didn't really want to explore it further. "Whatever's the

43

matter with Peter? I thought he was a lawyer and had good sense."

"Good sense doesn't always mean bravery," Emily mumbled. "I was jilted, that's all."

Mrs. Crane looked away as if Emily had said something disgraceful. Then she brightened. "It was only a week ago that you lost your job! You'll get another. Or maybe you'll meet some nice young man. Isn't there someone intriguing in your life?" Emily shook her head. "You're not getting any younger, Em. The men don't like women over thirty, you know."

It was an old contest between them, and Emily didn't have the energy to support her side. She wished she could talk about Jeff with her mother, but Mrs. Crane couldn't abide the memory, she said—too painful.

"I—I want you to have this," Mrs. Crane said, slipping a check across the table. "I know times are difficult."

Emily opened the folded check. It was fifty dollars. "Mother, you can't afford—"

"I had a good run at bridge last week," she said, her thin pretty lips turning up neatly at the corners. "Now, I really must go and catch that three-thirty train. Keep in touch," she said, and brushed her cheek against her daughter's. In seconds, she was moving away from the booth.

"Thank you, Mother," Emily said. Her mother waved without turning around. Emily slumped in the booth and accepted more coffee from the waitress. She came out of her thoughts when she recognized Sally, the vice-president of Liberty Watch. Her poodle cut had caught Emily's eye. Emily waved.

Sally veered around a table and came to rest beside Emily. She looked grim. "Hello," she said dully. "I suppose you've heard."

"Heard what?" asked Emily. "I've been looking for a job."

"About Ralph Metzger."

"Oh. Yes, he made some kind of deal with the committee and didn't have to testify. I was shocked. After all, he was the loudest—"

"No," Sally said. "He shot himself yesterday."

Stunned, Emily whispered, "Why?"

Sally sat down. Her nature had never been cheerful; delivering bad news suited her. "Because, well, his note said he had been shamed. He'd lost his courage. He had betrayed himself and his friends."

Metzger's suicide shocked them all, but coming on top of being fired from her job, Emily particularly found it hard to cope with the intensely human calamity. Reality as she had known it pitched and tilted. Her gloom deepened. She presented a sunny face to the world, but it became harder to maintain each day that she searched for a new job.

She had started with the big magazines— *Time* and *Life*—and had worked her way down to the Girl Scouts without a single offer. Her savings dropped steadily.

After three months, she'd finally taken a job as a clerk in a photo shop. It was only interim, she'd told herself. She'd been there a week when two FBI men had called on Janos, the owner of the shop. They'd worn dark suits, dark hats, and stiff faces. They'd just been leaving when she'd returned from lunch. They tipped their hats at her. Janos, an elderly man originally from Yugoslavia, had told her he was sorry, but he had decided he didn't need any more clerical help. He'd pressed a week's pay into her hand, and had turned his back. He'd been afraid.

She had reacquainted herself with her apartment on the upper West Side. Except for the weekends, she hadn't been in it during the day for years. The building was old but well cared for by Mrs. Solansky, who'd once been a tap dancer and "variety artist." She dyed her hair red and wore a large collection of rings on her chubby fingers. Emily liked her.

Emily's apartment was on the second floor—an airy living room, a rather dark but cozy bedroom, and a kitchen the size of a closet. A huge, claw-footed bathtub dominated the once rather grand bathroom. A narrow stained-glass window painted the room like a rainbow when the sun hit it in midmorning. The low bookcases in Emily's living room were crammed with all her college texts as well as novels, histories, and design books. A Toulouse-Lautrec print hung over one end of a bookcase near the window that looked out on the street. Her furniture was an odd assortment, but when jumbled together gave her space a quiet charm. Emily had a good eye and was an inveterate Saturday shopper in the antique and secondhand stores on Third Avenue.

Liberty, the kitten she'd found at the Dworkins' the day she'd been subpoenaed, was now half grown, demure and self-centered. She kept her white chest spotless. Gray and black stripes wound around her sides and coiled about her proud tail. Her post was at the front window, looking down on the street.

Liberty was sometimes the only living thing Emily saw all day. For a while after the photostore incident, she didn't have the heart to go job hunting. But for the most part, Emily kept her spirits up gamely. Occasionally, on the street in front of the *LOOK* building, she'd meet people from the office where she'd made so many friends—or so she'd believed. Tommy stopped to chat for a moment, but he was always in a hurry so she understood when he rushed off. She found it harder when others passed her with a quick smile, but didn't break their pace or ask how she was.

In July, she'd found a job as a file clerk at the picture bureau of the Associated Press. She had just begun to settle in when the same two FBI men had materialized from nowhere. She'd been fired that afternoon. She called Alan and told him about the FBI men who kept following her around and losing her hard-won jobs for her.

"They want you to give them the Liberty Watch membership lists, Emily. They want you to break with us. It's simple harassment."

"I'm not going to do it," she said.

It was after she'd lost the AP job that she began to look behind her when she walked on the street or rode a bus. An uneasy mantle of suspicion settled on her and she couldn't shake it. She started smoking a pack of cigarettes a day.

On the day she was turned down as a file clerk in a picture magazine in the Village, she broke. She had just come inside her apartment and closed the door when she began crying. She had done everything she could think of to get a job, and nothing was working. She sat down heavily on the couch, and wept. Liberty sat in the window, staring at her. Emily had never felt so low.

The next morning, she forced herself to get out of bed. She had decided that she would look for a job outside her field—then perhaps the FBI would leave her alone. To get her spirits back up, she put on the prettiest dress she owned and a new strand of pop-it beads that she'd bought as a treat. "You're going to beat this thing," she told herself in the mirror as she put on her lipstick. "You are not going to sink beneath the waves."

It was a summer morning, warm and balmy, not really hot yet. Emily skipped down the steps of her modest, old apartment building and took a deep breath of the air. It smelled like the sea, but she could tell that in a couple of hours, it would be hot. She shifted the rolled-up newspaper under her arm and swung out onto the sidewalk.

Suddenly, the two FBI men who were so expert at appearing out of thin air were planted right in front of her. She particularly disliked the looks of the younger one.

"You again," she said. "Is it part of your technique to just drop from the skies like this?"

"Miss Crane?" Cochran asked politely. She looked very pretty and innocent in the yellow dress that set off her complexion and hair. He showed her his badge. "Special Agent Cochran, Federal Bureau of Investigation. We'd like to talk to you, please."

"I've nothing to say to you," she replied, head up, already walking past them. "I want you to quit bothering me."

"Miss Crane, you refused to supply the Congress with certain information that is vital to the U.S. security," Hackett said in an official monotone.

"That's my right, as I hear it," said Emily. She didn't stop walking and didn't turn around.

Cochran and Hackett looked after her. "Legs still holding up," said Cochran. She seemed to dance as she walked, bouncy but graceful.

On Broadway, she saw Warren Barringer coming toward her. She hadn't seen him for four months, and in that time she'd swung between anger and compassion for him. But he wasn't her enemy; she knew that he would have been fired, too, if he'd tried to protect her. He couldn't have prevented her from losing her job. She waved her hand and smiled tentatively.

Warren saw her but he didn't smile. He glanced around. Emily picked up her pace. He looked trapped, and then, when only a few yards remained between them, he stumbled off the curb and crossed to the island by the subway station. Emily looked after him, feeling desperately alone. Her cheerful mood vanished; a furious sadness swamped her.

"I hope you remember that," Marilyn said to her later that morning. They were sitting on a bench in a playground, watching Marilyn's small son, Jerry. He climbed up a slide, slid down, and then, shrieking with delight, ran around and did it again. "I *always* said Warren Beringer was a rat."

"I still thought he was my friend," Emily said sadly. "I just can't get over it."

"With friends like that—" Marilyn broke off when she saw what Jerry was about to do. "Feet-first, Jerry!" she called out. "You go down a slide feet-first!"

"Why?" Jerry demanded. He was a pugnacious, sturdy child. Alan had said, half joking, that Jerry would make a good criminal lawyer when he grew up.

"Because your mother says so, that's why." Marilyn turned back to Emily. "Forget about Warren. Anything on the job front?"

Emily unrolled her newspaper. "I saw something listed this morning. It's out in Brooklyn."

Marilyn groaned. "That's such a shlep."

"Maybe the FBI doesn't know how to get to Brooklyn," Emily said, smiling, her spirits lifting a little.

Marilyn peered at Emily. "I hate to see you like this, Emily. So cheerful," she said sarcastically. "I mean, you find some lousy, rotten, underpaid job you're way too good for, and then the FBI shows up, scares the owner, and you get canned. I'd be kicking and screaming. But you—you just tuck it away somewhere and keep on smiling. How do you do it?"

When Emily smiled, her whole face lifted and her eyes flashed deliciously. But she couldn't quite make her smile work this morning. "I grind my teeth at night," Emily said as she lit a cigarette. "Does that make you feel better?"

"No."

"I'm smoking again," she said, waving her cigarette in Marilyn's direction. "I'm reading books I always meant to read. I stay home a lot. Men ask me out but—" Very slowly her smile vanished. "But I don't feel—you'll laugh at me. I don't feel very attractive these days. That's funny, isn't it?"

"It is for you! Better go out with them. They'll change your mind in a hurry." Marilyn had known Emily for nearly ten years, and in all that time, she'd never seen Emily as depressed as when Pete wouldn't answer her phone calls right after she was fired. She'd taken a terrible double blow and she wasn't over it yet.

"A lot of the time," Emily continued, leaning back on the bench, "I feel guilty. That's another strange thing, isn't it? I know what I did. I worked for a good cause that's out of favor—to put it mildly. And then I told Congress—can you imagine?—that I thought doing that work was right, not wrong, and that I wouldn't give them what they wanted. And I'd do it again. Now, why should I feel guilty?"

"You took on the government. Big Daddy. You defied them. It."

"I say to myself, 'Feel mad, not guilty.' It doesn't help."

"Mommy! Look!" yelled Jerry.

"There goes my son," Marilyn said, "right on his head."

They watched as Jerry started to slide down headfirst.

"Shouldn't you stop him?" Emily asked, uneasily.

Marilyn sighed. "He might as well learn now."

Jerry landed on his head and then stood up unhurt, smiling and triumphant.

"He's just like you," Marilyn observed dryly.

Emily let out a peal of musical laughter. It was tough not to laugh with her, but somehow Marilyn refrained. "Look," Marilyn said seriously, "why don't you come over this afternoon? We can have a good chat, like in the old days when we never thought about the FBI."

"No thanks, I'm off to find my fortune in Brooklyn," Emily said briskly. She hugged Marilyn.

"Brooklyn," said Marilyn, shaking her shoulders as if she were cold under the warm sun. "The whole idea gives me the creeps. Do you know where you're going?"

"No," Emily said simply. "I don't."

In fact, Emily had checked the subway map but she could only guess at the correct station. She got off on President Street.

When she came up out of the subway, the shouts of exuberant children filled the air as they clustered around a Good Humor truck. The street was lined with old row houses that had once been elegant. The balustrades edging their stairs were hand-carved, and some of the windows held flower boxes or intricate Victorian fretwork. A few were freshly painted. But the neighborhood was sad and dilapidated. She felt the urge to turn back, get away. The sun was bright, the children high-spirited, even rough with their friends, but the neighborhood wasn't just down-and-out—it seemed sinister.

She shook herself out of her mood and watched a thin boy of about sixteen walking toward her. He was eating an ice cream bar. He had light brown hair and large eyes. Suddenly, high above her head, she heard a bird cry out— sharp and shrill, a scream, really. The boy ducked instinctively, his face full of terror and surprise. He dropped his ice cream. The bird screamed on. The boy looked like a rabbit hunting for a hiding place.

The bird's persistent shriek was like a warning, and it had startled Emily, too. She shaded her eyes against the sunlight. The bird, much larger than a pigeon, was swooping down from a roof, wings out, gaining speed. At the last moment, it pulled out of its dive just above Emily and the boy, peeling off gracefully and climbing away into the sun.

"What was that?" she asked the youth. He was trembling violently. Shaken, she shaded her eyes again, looking for the mysterious and threatening bird. "Was that a hawk?"

"Maybe," he said, looking at her miserably.

"It dive-bombed us!" she said. "What's a hawk doing in Brooklyn?" He shook his head as if he didn't understand. "Oh, never mind," she said. The children were still leaping around the ice cream truck, shouting out their orders. The young man moved off.

"Excuse me," she said, rushing after him. She unrolled her newspaper and looked for the ad she'd marked. "Please?" she called to him. He stopped. She showed him the newspaper ad. "Can you tell me where this street is?" He had clear gray eyes, and his face was pale. He was very thin.

He peered at the ad and then pointed.

"It is same like this street," he said in a European accent. "Same—as, uh—" He couldn't find the English expression and said something in his native tongue, holding out his hands to demonstrate what he meant.

"Parallel?" Emily asked.

"Yes! Is parallel!" he said, pleased. "Around corner, you go left, is first street parallel."

"Thank you," she said.

"Stefan."

A handsome woman stood in the doorway to the nearest row house, holding the door open. He instantly broke away from Emily.

"Yes, Matilde," he said, and climbed the steps to the front door. The woman eyed Emily as if she were memorizing her features. The boy glanced at Matilde nervously; he was clearly ashamed to be caught talking to strangers. As soon as he was inside, the woman shut the door with a bang.

Emily followed Stefan's instructions and found herself looking up at a row of brownstones that looked just like the ones on the street she'd just been on. She checked the address on her paper, found the right house, and rang the doorbell. A maid opened it and looked out at her suspiciously.

"I came about the job," Emily said politely.

"You're too early," the maid snapped. "The ad said two o'clock."

Emily had come a long way and she was not about to twiddle her thumbs in some coffee shop or stand around on a corner until two. With her best smile she said, "Oh, please?"

The maid sighed and opened the door another inch so that Emily could just barely squeeze inside. "Wait," she said unceremoniously, and disappeared.

The foyer was in the Victorian style with a fine fruitwood staircase and banister even though its carpet treads were worn. A single frosted-glass light fixture in the shape of delicate leaves hung from the ceiling by an ornamental chain. The house smelled of wax and sweetly perfumed soap.

"You may come," said the maid, reappearing suddenly.

She led Emily into a large, dark, overdecorated room filled with turn-of-the-century furniture, stuffed and tasseled cushions, doilies, framed pictures large and small, flowered wallpaper, oriental throw rugs, colored and painted lamps, side chairs. There wasn't a single open or empty space anywhere in the room.

At first glance, Emily didn't see the old woman, she was so busy taking in the junky antique festival that littered the room. But at an abrupt gesture from the maid, Emily discovered the lady's white hair and wizened face. She was sitting in an ornate, stuffed chair near a small round table whose surface was crowded with mementos. Her chair was a real period piece. Its ball-and-claw feet dug into the frayed carpet.

"This is Miss Venable," said the maid as she left.

"I came about the job," Emily said. "My name is Emily Crane." She was trying to adjust her eyes to the warm, dim, and gloomy room. The curtains were drawn against the summer light. Miss Venable apparently didn't feel warm, for her dark dress came up to her throat where a large cameo pin fastened it. She was small and looked like a feisty bird someone had abandoned.

"Well, at least you've got spunk coming early," Miss Venable said. Her voice was as wrinkled as her face. She sounded tight-lipped and crusty, as if warmth or human sympathy were as passé as her furnishings. "I guess you're not afraid of being turned away."

"I need the job," Emily said simply.

Miss Venable reached for a book sitting on the little knick-knack-laden table. Emily noticed Miss Venable's long bony fingers and her sapphire rings. "Read this," she directed, handing Emily the book.

Still standing in the middle of the room, her newspaper rolled under her arm, Emily opened

the book and squinted at the print in the dim
light.

"To me," Miss Venable quipped, cackling
softly.

Emily smiled as she glanced at the first page—
Miss Venable's tastes ran to very trashy ro-
mances. Then she began to read in a clear, even
voice:

"'His wild, dark looks thrilled Marissa to her
very marrow. His eyes glinted at her, sweeping
over her body like a brush. She felt her heart
leaping behind her breast at the thought that
such a handsome man, even if he had no station
in life, would even look at her. What fate, she
wondered, had driven her—'"

"That will be enough," said Miss Venable. "I
think you will do. Your voice has a certain
cultivation. Have you been to college?" she
asked.

"Yes, Miss Venable," Emily said politely.

"Did you graduate?"

"Yes." And Emily felt compelled to add, "Cum
laude."

Unimpressed, Miss Venable continued. "My
eyes have begun to fail. I require someone to
read to me. Your hours will be determined by
how I feel, night or day." She sighed, and
reached into her sleeve for a lace handkerchief.
Out in the hall, Emily heard a faint slap as if the
maid had dropped a magazine. Miss Venable
squeezed her eyes shut. "There are times when
the slightest sound is unbearable." She opened
her eyes and peered at Emily. "The salary will
be fifty dollars a week."

"That's not very much," Emily said boldly.

Miss Venable appraised Emily critically. "The door is right behind you." She held out her hand for the book, then, conceding slightly, she added, "You will also be fed."

After a moment, Emily said, "When do I start?"

"Now."

The book was called *Wild Winds*. It took place in Georgian England. Reginald, the hero, was a duke disguised as a ship's captain; Marissa Wakefield was an orphan, a governess, traveling to a distant port to take up her new employment with, as it was to be revealed, the duke's family. Emily read several chapters of the book that afternoon, keeping her tone slow and quiet, yet expressive, especially in the more colorful sections that came every twenty pages or so:

" 'His arms embraced her passionately and his lips pressed against hers possessively. She trembled against him, and felt a shiver cut through her like a wand. She knew she was his forever as his hand slipped inside her bodice and nuzzled her breast. She felt her breath pulled out of her by the force of his passion. She reached her arms around his broad shoulders. She ached to kiss him again. . . .' "

Emily suppressed a smile as she glanced at the prim and small Miss Venable, sitting up so straight in her chair, listening to *Wild Winds'* hot, shallow narrative. She didn't seem to be self-conscious or embarrassed about her choice of literature but bent her head in attention as if

Emily were reading *The Mill on The Floss* or the morning newspaper.

The maid brought her a glass of lemonade and, at four o'clock, a small slice of cake.

As Emily read on, she wondered if she should warn Miss Venable about what the FBI might say to her should they arrive on her doorstep. But Emily put the prospect aside. Inside the Venable establishment the FBI seemed like a government bureau yet to be created, so complete was the nineteenth-century aura of the room. It held her as firmly in its walls as it held all the accumulated objects of Miss Venable's long life.

At five o'clock, Miss Venable waved her thin, clawlike hand. "Enough," she whispered. "Come at eleven o'clock tomorrow."

"Yes, Miss Venable," Emily said, rising as noiselessly as she could and tiptoeing out of the dim, overstuffed room.

Outside on the street, she allowed herself a good laugh. Four months ago, as she poured over photos of soldiers with their mad, cowed eyes, how could she have known that she'd be reading trashy novels to a Victorian lady in Brooklyn? She was grinning like an idiot. Life was strange indeed. A couple of children pointed at her.

The next day, Emily picked up where she'd left off:

"'Marissa, you are everything I desire,' said Reginald. He stood against the bow of the ship, his broad shoulders against the sky, his head cocked. 'Do not say anything, my love,' he said, reaching out for her and drawing her to his

chest. He lifted her chin and kissed her passionately. She withdrew. His kisses left her feeling
weak with desire. 'No,' she said, 'we mustn't.'
Her greatest fear was to be parted from him
once they reached port. She knew she was just a
dalliance for him. Reginald's response was to
pick her up and carry her below, away from the
silvery eyes of the moon.

"Making love at last was the most perfect
moment of her existence. She was swimming in
Reginald's arms, throbbing with the desire he
kindled. His lips pressed against her naked
breast, his hand—"

Emily paused. Miss Venable had fallen asleep.
She put the book down and slipped out of the
dark, heavy room into the bright foyer.

In the kitchen, Alma, the maid, looked up
from her magazine. "She'll wake up and wonder
where you are. Cranky, she is," said the maid.

"Can I get to the garden from here?" asked
Emily.

"Sure, go down the backstairs," Alma said
with a twitch of her head. She was sullen and
had little pouty lips.

Emily looked down into the brilliantly sunlit
garden below. Like so many New York neighbor-
hoods, each house had its own back garden so
that, from her vantage point, the gardens
formed a chain of rectangles down the inner
block. She went down the rickety backstairs.
The garden was quiet and very peaceful. Miss
Venable's property was separated from the backyard of the house behind it by an old, bleached
wooden fence. A trumpet vine trailed over one

section of it, then fell away in a section un-
friendly to vines.

The day was hot and muggy; windows were
open. Emily could hear someone expertly practicing piano scales mixed with the murmur of
floating voices. She sat down on the bench, lit a
cigarette, and relaxed into the summer day. She
closed her eyes.

A loud, angry voice speaking in what sounded
like German jerked her out of her reverie.

"He says it is too dangerous, that he's been
here long enough, and that, uh, promises have
been made. He says he will not be treated like
this!" a young voice translated.

The voices were coming from the house opposite Miss Venable's. They obliterated the sounds
of the children and the piano. Then they
stopped. But just as Emily relaxed again, the
German voice began again, yelling, followed by
the words of the anxious translator.

"He does not feel safe in this—city. He wants
to be moved. . . ."

"Dr. Teperson knows what we're waiting for,"
said a third male voice.

There was something familiar to Emily about
this last voice. The parlor-floor windows of the
house were open and she could now see the
figure of an old man, who was still speaking in
German. He was pacing back and forth. Curious, Emily stood up and walked slowly toward
the fence that divided Miss Venable's property
from the other house. She pushed aside some
shrubbery to get a better view. She was surprised to see the boy—Stefan—who had given

her directions on the street come into view as he moved toward the man who called himself Teperson. Excitedly, Mr. Teperson went on in German and Stefan continued to translate to the unseen man. "He wishes to know about his assistants."

"Tell Dr. Teperson not to worry. They're coming," the man answered. He moved past a curtain and came into view. Emily clapped a hand over her mouth. It was Samuel Salwen from the committee!

Emily couldn't believe her eyes. What on earth was he doing there?

Salwen had his hand jammed into the pockets of his beautiful suit. He was saying affably, "Tell him Rome wasn't built in a day. The assistants will be here, I guarantee. There was a little problem getting them out. It's all fixed now."

Emily saw Salwen grin and put his arm around the shoulder of the older man. Then he whispered something; Teperson nodded and smiled tightly. Salwen whispered again and Teperson chuckled. A phone rang somewhere in the house. Salwen looked at Teperson as though they shared a mutual secret, then he disappeared from view.

Still chuckling, Teperson went to the open window that faced the garden, spread his arms wide, taking a deep breath of the fragrant air. He was short, with a potbelly and close-cropped white hair. He used choppy, demanding gestures as if he were used to giving orders.

He saw Emily and his smile vanished. Emily,

transfixed, stared back at him. Abruptly, he slammed the window shut.

After she had finished reading to Miss Venable that evening, Emily walked along Carroll Street, counting the houses until she came to the one opposite Miss Venable's. It was, as many were, a Victorian brownstone with stone steps and peeling cream-colored paint. She couldn't get over the remarkable coincidence of seeing Salwen at the window. Salwen was the last man she thought she'd meet again. It was so eerie that she felt chilled to the bone and clutched her handbag tightly to her side.

As she looked up at the old house, she didn't notice that someone was staring at her from the second-story window.

Chapter 4

Liberty was extremely pleased to see Emily that evening when she got back to her apartment. She wound between Emily's legs, then dashed ahead to the little kitchen and looked up at the pint-sized refrigerator. "It's shameful," said Emily, "the way you make me cater to you."

After she fed Liberty, Emily put something called a TV dinner in the oven. "It's new," she said to Liberty who was paying no attention but eating rapidly and with concentration. "You eat it while you watch television."

While it was baking, she showered and got into her nightgown. The day's adventures with Marissa and Reggie had exhausted her. She put the TV dinner on a tray and carried it into her bedroom. Liberty climbed into the little boudoir chair, sat down, and began her afterdinner wash.

Emily puffed up the pillows around her on the bed and turned on her ten-inch black-and-white TV set. Thomas Boyle's popular weekly televi-

sion show was in progress. Boyle was known as
an interviewer who "went for the throat." Senator Byington, the featured guest, sat in a molded
plastic chair regarding his host. Boyle's guests
endured his snide remarks and irritating inter-
ruptions in exchange for exposure to large
American audiences. Peter had said to Emily
that he thought guests went on the Boyle show
to meet the challenge of "besting Boyle." Whatever the reason, Boyle never had a shortage of
cannon fodder for the show—opinion makers all.

"See?" she pointed out to Liberty. "There's a
senator I've actually had words with." She tentatively stuck a fork in a brown mass at two
o'clock on her plate.

Byington was holding his own in the type of
interview few survived. His manner was sincere and impressive. "I think it's most important," he said, leaning forward, a frown of
intelligent concern lining his brow, "that we
don't lose sight of why we fought the war. It's
easy to do these days. The enemy has changed,
we're under attack from a different quarter. But
we fought for certain principles and we can't
forget them."

"You mean, the four freedoms. Things like
that," snapped Boyle, summarizing. Boyle's eyebrows rode sharply in the middle like upright
triangles, but his mouth turned down. He rarely
took his eyes off his guests, which had brought
one reviewer to remark that Boyle's focus resembled a lion in the tall grass watching an
antelope.

"Yes, the four freedoms, things exactly like that," Senator Byington replied. "But what I want to get across is that we have to be careful."

"God, this is terrible," Emily muttered, tasting her food.

"About what, Senator?" asked Boyle, looking up from his notes sharply. "Let's be precise."

"Now, Thomas," said Byington, smiling with considerable charm, "you know better than to ask a politician to be precise."

Boyle did not return the smile, but his grim, flinty, intelligent face lightened minutely. "What exactly do you think we have to be careful about, Senator?"

"Well, who was it said, 'Our reliance is in the love of liberty which God has planted in us'?" Byington asked.

Boyle bit, succumbing to an excess of zeal: "Jefferson?" he guessed.

"Lincoln, you jerk," Emily answered out loud.

"No . . . I don't think so," Byington said to Boyle. "It was Lincoln, I believe, in one of his campaign speeches." He looked up at Boyle. "We have to be on guard we don't lose that liberty. That's our most precious possession," he went on, warming up to the concept of liberty. "Not guns, not great factories, not wealth . . . but freedom. That's what makes this country great."

Emily nodded reluctantly. She didn't want to, but she was beginning to like this man who had sat in judgment on her at the hearing.

"I can see it now!" exclaimed Boyle. "You're going to make that one of your campaign—"

"Now, Thomas," Byington cut in skillfully, "you know I'm not running for any other office."

"Not yet," Boyle said, with a cold smile.

"I haven't started any campaign," the senator insisted.

"That's evasive," said Boyle, pitching himself forward. He was trying to figure out how to get Byington to reveal his plans. "But you're thinking—"

"I'm always thinking," said Byington with a smile. Boyle's theme music was coming up; the show was over.

Emily turned off the TV set. She was proud to own it, even if she were paying for it in installments. She took the unappetizing TV dinner back to the kitchen and put it down for Liberty. She returned to her bedroom, fluffed up the pillows and fell back on them. *What a day,* she thought. She turned out the lights and felt Liberty leap onto the bed.

Why had Salwen been in New York, in *Brooklyn* at that? And what had Salwen meant when he said, "They're coming?" *Who* was coming? From where? Why didn't Dr. Teperson—had that been his name?—feel safe? She found herself reliving her hearing, clenching inside at Salwen's masterfully condescending and shocking innuendos that even now, in the dark privacy of her bedroom, made her cringe. She remembered his boredom with her toward the end when he saw she wasn't going to give in or cry or break. She was proud of that. She saw Salwen whispering to Byington as he was about to cut his absurd birthday cake. And she remembered how close they'd seemed, how connected. The whole puzzle intrigued her yet it made her feel vulnerable and faintly alarmed.

"That's silly, isn't it, Liberty?" she mumbled in the dark.

The next day was overcast and humid. As Emily climbed the stairs to Miss Venable's, the front door swung open. Cochran and Hackett stood above her just inside the vestibule. Her heart sank at the sight of them.

"Oh, no," she said.

"Ready to talk to us, Miss Crane?" Cochran asked pleasantly.

"Is this what you do to law-abiding, working people in this country?" she demanded. "You're —you're harassing me!"

"Now, Miss Crane—" Hackett began, but Cochran put a hand on his arm.

"I just get a job and then you lose it for me!"

Cochran saw her face become vibrant with outrage and fear. A splinter of compassion went through him. To cover the feeling, he shrugged. They passed her on their way down the steps.

Emily watched their retreating backs as they strode down the street in lock step. *Right, left, right, left,* she thought. Why didn't they leave her alone? She felt like crying.

"Miss Crane?" It was Miss Venable calling her.

Emily broke out of her thoughts and darted inside the gloomy house. The scent of soap and wax greeted her as she made her way quickly to Miss Venable's dark, ornate chamber. Miss

Venable was seated in the wing-back chair. A soft spill of light from the gaudy, old-fashioned lamp covered her like a golden shawl.

"You're late," Miss Venable said.

"I'm sorry they bothered you," Emily began. She braced herself for the inevitable dismissal.

"They did not bother me," the old lady said, annoyed. "They disturbed me, Miss Crane. I dislike being disturbed." Emily noticed that Miss Venable had very sharp, alert eyes.

"I should have told you—" Emily apologized.

"I have no interest in your troubles, Miss Crane," Miss Venable retorted, waving a bony hand as if to divert a fly from her face.

"Do you want me to leave?"

"You will be informed when I do. Please continue reading."

Emily sank down in her flowered chair. "Thank you. Thank you very much," Emily said gratefully. Suddenly she felt terribly lonely. She wanted to tell Miss Venable all the reasons she'd ended up reading to her in this dark, festooned house, wanted to tell her about how much she'd loved her job at *LOOK* magazine. She wanted to share the questions that assailed her about seeing Salwen in the house across the garden—

"Well?" Miss Venable said, her voice as brittle as a stick.

Emily picked up the book, opened it to her place, and began reading about Reggie's well-matted chest as he worked on the three-masted schooner. Marissa had been delivered to her charges at the duke's estate out in the country, had met the children, and the somber, bitter old duke who was dying of a lung disease. "But her every thought was of Reggie, 'the buchaneer captain' who had taken her heart by storm. Marissa thought back to their lovemaking her last night on board the ship, of the feeling that she was splintering deliciously from silver sensations as she rode in his arms. She could still feel the taste of his lips and his warm breath rushing past her ear."

The summer day was as ordinary and calm as a bathtub full of warm water. Emily went into the garden for lunch. But as she surreptitiously looked up at the windows of the house in which she'd seen Salwen the day before, all her curiosity and misgivings returned: the shades were drawn. She heard the children on the far street, a small dog yapping, and the buzzing of some bees around Miss Venable's tea roses. But from that house on Carroll Street—nothing. It was as if she'd dreamed the loud argument yesterday.

Emily read to Miss Venable until almost five o'clock that afternoon, taking Marissa through the shock of finding Reggie at the banquet, his sister's jealousy, the unexpected arrival of Reggie's mother from court, a grotesque picnic party, and a lovemaking episode in the gazebo of Reggie's family estate.

Coming out of Miss Venable's house was like reentering the twentieth century, just as going in in the morning was like leaving reality, and this century, behind. But in other ways, Emily found the shelter of the Venable establishment soothing. It was a respite from the rough seas that had brought her there in the first place.

The sensation of passing from one time frame to another was accentuated by the romance spasms in the lurid book. What was it that Miss Venable got out of these stories? They were nearly finished with Marissa and Reggie. What fine piece of literature would they turn to next? Emily wondered. Even though Miss Venable remained distinctly mute throughout their sessions, Emily was beginning to realize that the old lady was much more perspicacious than she'd seemed at first. The FBI had not put her off her stride for a moment.

Emily was buying a newspaper at a corner stand when she saw Stefan talking to the short, dark woman called Matilde. They hadn't seen Emily but were deep in conversation. Matilde might have been thirty or fifty. She had deep creases around her mouth, but her skin was smooth and translucently beautiful. Her dark hair was short and wavy. Her skirt was fashionably midcalf-length, and the collar of her bright blue summer jacket was turned up smartly. Yet there was something that told Emily the woman hadn't had money for such nice clothes all her life. She was too conscious of the way she looked in them. She ran her hand down the jacket to make sure it was smooth, and she inched away from a boy to protect her skirt from his ice cream cone. Matilde was shaking her finger at Stefan. Then she patted his cheek roughly and strode off rapidly across the street in her sensible but nevertheless fashionable shoes.

When she was out of earshot, Emily went up to Stefan. "Hello," she said.

Stefan looked at her, puzzled.

"We met the other day, remember?" asked Emily. "I asked you for an address." She held out her hands. "Parallel?"

"Oh, yes! You have found the house?" he said, remembering.

"Yes, thank you." Emily smiled in a way she knew to be very attractive. She wanted to keep the conversation going but she didn't know quite how to do that. Conversation with this boy was labored under any conditions. "Do you live in the neighborhood?" she asked.

He cocked his head like a bird who'd heard a sound that put him on guard. He didn't answer. In an effort to lull his suspicions, she said, "I work just around the corner. I was looking for a job at that address. When I asked you to help me." She kept her voice light and neutral. "The job is reading."

That perked up his interest and seemed to allay his suspicion. He pointed to a book sticking out of her purse.

"You are a reader?" he asked.

"Yes, I read aloud. Not this book, though. This one's for my own pleasure."

"May I see it?" he asked.

"Yes, of course," Emily said as she pulled the book out of her purse and handed it to him. He had long, narrow fingers.

"Dickinson . . . Dickinson," he said, looking at the cover. "Should I know about this Dickinson?"

"She's a wonderful poet," Emily smiled. "I'm named after her."

"You are name of Dickinson?" he asked, not understanding.

"My first name. Emily," she explained. "My full name is Emily Crane." She offered her hand, but he was taking a small book with a red cover out of his pocket. He didn't introduce himself. "What's your name?" she asked.

"Oh." He saw her hand and touched it gingerly with his own. "Stefan Hudak," he said.

"I am pleased to meet you, Stefan," she said.

"Do you know a Mr. Edgar Allan Poe?" he asked, almost as though he thought it possible that Emily was Poe's friend.

"Oh, yes," Emily said, pushing some excitement into her voice.

"I practice English with his poems," Stefan said, almost bashfully. "For the sound, you know?" He attempted a smile and almost made it. 'The tintinnabulation of the bells, bells, bells,' he recited perfectly. "I think that is very beautiful sound, no?"

"Very beautiful," Emily said, suppressing a smile. It was odd yet amusing to stand on a worn-out old Brooklyn Street listening to a timid but appealing foreigner recite Poe. "You speak English very well. Where did you learn?" she asked.

"Many places," Stefan said, on guard again.

"During the war?" Emily said trying to sound interested but not prying.

"During. After." He was stuffing the book back in his pocket.

"Are you a translator? Is that what you do?" she asked, taking a chance.

"Why do you think that?" Stefan asked her.

Emily did not see the extent of his wary distrust. She was caught up in her need to know more about him, more about Salwen and the Sullivan Street house. "Because I heard you translating the other day. I mean, I couldn't help it. The window was open and that other man was yelling."

Stefan's expression went completely blank. "What man?"

"The man who was so angry," Emily said hesitantly. "Dr. Teperson. The short man who sounded German."

"You saw him," Stefan said flatly.

"I'm sorry," Emily said, trying to sound abashed and harmless. "I didn't mean to—"

"You know German?" he asked, completely focused on her. "You understand?"

Emily shook her head. "I had enough trouble in Latin and I'm not very—"

"Do you know this name—Teperson?" he pressed her. His brow was pinched into an anxious frown.

Cautiously she said, "No. Should I?"

"Thank you for your Dickinson," he said stiffly, and handed her back her book.

He turned to leave. Her chance was slipping away. "Do you translate for Mr. Salwen?" she tried rashly, not caring now how agitated the question might make him.

Stefan stopped, his back to her. He did not turn around. His voice was utterly devoid of expression. "I do not know a Mr. Salwen."

"But I saw—" The words were out of her mouth before Emily realized that she'd gone too far. But too far for what? What was going on in the house? Who was this young boy with the pianist's hands, and why was Salwen with them?

Slowly, Stefan turned to her. He said emphatically, "You are making a mistake. Excuse me, please. Goodbye."

Emily watched him walk rapidly away, without once looking back at her. Stefan intrigued her, but his fear was so palpable, so unsettling. And Stefan, she now knew, was certainly afraid. It looked like the only emotion he'd been able to count on for a long time.

The house on Carroll Street was furnished with second hand goods that had had no style even when new. The living room looked like a way-station, a place people met other people they didn't know well.

"But, Matilde!" Stefan whined, "I know nothing of her!" Matilde's hand snapped forward like an adder to slap him hard across the face. "Matilde! I know nothing!" he wailed. He bent over at the waist, holding his cheek. He was trembling from head to foot.

Stefan hated arguments because they led to pain and violence and death. He had seen all those and more in the war. No part of him believed he'd escaped that dark agony. Once in a while, a tiny spirt of hope rushed through him; once in a very great while a stab of memory punctured him: his sixth birthday in a large sunny house in Warsaw, or a strand of piano music, or his mother lifting her long hair and pinning it to her head with a tortoiseshell comb.

Matilde's sharp dark eyes looked at him fiercely, calculating belief. On the other side of the dingy dining room, leaning against the doorjamb to the kitchen, a short, muscular man named McKay watched them. He had a closed face that looked perpetually sleepy—a terrible deceit. He was alert at all times and moved with the spring of an athlete. He was Matilde's satellite. McKay was as menacing as anyone Stefan had known in the camps.

"You talked to her long enough!" Matilde snapped.

"Poems . . . we talked of poems! She is a reader!" Stefan cried, trying to explain. He kept his eye on McKay. Stefan was in agony. Matilde did not read and would not understand.

"What else did she say?" Matilde demanded.

"Nothing! I have told you—"

"I brought you over and I can send you back," she said.

"Please, no! I am telling the truth!"

The two of them looked at him doubtfully. Then Matilde broke away and went over to the breakfront and opened a drawer.

"Emily Crane?" she said again.

Stefan nodded. "She is named for poet Dickinson."

Matilde turned. She evaluated him shrewdly, then shut the drawer with a crack, went to the phone, and started dialing. "We'll see," she said.

Salwen's law offices were on the fourth floor of a new building on Connecticut Avenue in Washington, D.C. For his work with the committee, he had been alotted additional space adjacent to Byington's offices in the Capitol building.

Salwen bounded out of bed that morning and started a vigorous exercise routine that included twenty push-ups—a habit he'd gotten into during his days in the marines. He had a single glass of orange juice and some crisp bacon while he read the *Washington Post*. He selected a charcoal-gray suit of a light summer weight, a white shirt, and a pink tie—a new fashion color for men. Salwen dressed expensively and with a shrewd eye for new trends. Tucking *The New York Times* under his arm, he drove to his legal offices on Connecticut Avenue. He was halfway up the stairs, swinging his briefcase, when Ed Binney, his major aide, waved to him from the landing.

"Sam, wait!" Ed started toward him. They met in the middle. "It got here about a half hour ago," Ed said, pleased that he could look so efficient this early in the morning. Salwen could be a son-of-a-bitch, riding his staff mercilessly.

Binney handed Salwen a folder. Inside, several photos of a young woman were pasted to cardboard rectangles. Salwen took one and turned it over. On the back, in neat printing, it read, "Emily Crane—Property of the Federal Bureau of Investigation."

"Well, well, Miss Crane," Salwen whispered. "We meet again."

Chapter 5

Most of the offices for agents in the FBI building in New York City were small partitioned spaces. If looked at from above, the arena resembled a huge grid.

Hackett and Cochran's space was big enough for two beat-up gray metal desks, three chairs, and a battered four-drawer file cabinet. A day after Salwen opened Emily's FBI file, Mike Cochran was bending over the paperwork on his desk, applying himself diligently. Hackett sat at the other desk, slowly drawing a pencil down the edge of a ruler. He was turning a sheet of paper into columns.

"You working on this one?"

The director of the New York section, Ron Balone, tossed a file of photographs down on Hackett's desk. Hackett peered at the tab; it was Emily Crane's file. He opened it and spread the pictures.

"Yeah. Spot checking . . . see if she'll talk. Routine." Hackett said. Cochran craned his neck to get a look at the file. Then he saw one of the pictures he'd taken of the stubborn and beautiful Emily Crane.

"Lean on her," said Balone. He was a muscular man in his fifties who had served as a colonel in the peacetime army and still kept his rigid military bearing.

"Why? She's nothing special," protested Hackett.

"Washington wants it. Maybe she's hooked into something bigger," Ron Balone explained. His bushy eyebrows opposed his slicked-back hair and his sharply pressed suit.

"Like what?" Cochran wanted to know.

"Like go and find out," their boss replied as he marched out the door.

Cochran picked up one of Emily's pictures and looked at it. "I wonder what's up?" he muttered.

"Who cares?" Hackett groaned. "Stay outta it, Mike, I mean it. She's a pinko." He went back to his ruler and his pencil.

Stefan got off the subway, crossed the street to a pair of gilded, wrought-iron gates—the entrance to a cemetery—walked through them, and disappeared behind an ornate crypt surrounded by many tombstones. Emily was a short distance behind him.

It had started that afternoon as an exciting game. She had finished the saga of Reggie and Marissa when Reggie disclosed his true identity to his dying father and unmasked his stepmother. Miss Venable pronounced herself satisfied by Marissa's nuptials, and Emily had left the nineteenth century early. Walking over to Carroll

Street on an impulse, she'd caught sight of
Stefan hustling out the door of the house, carrying a couple of brimming garbage bags. A trash
can was sitting on the curb in front of the house,
but he ignored it, walking on down the street.
Curious, she'd followed at a distance. It was
easy to keep him in sight for there were only a
few people on the sidewalks. When he'd neared
the corner, he'd left one sack of garbage in the
trash can of a house several doors away from his
own. He'd deposited the other sack across the
street. Furtively, he'd glanced around again, but
he hadn't seen her because she'd ducked behind
a parked car.

Stefan had taken the subway next, and she'd
followed. Now she stood near the cemetery gatehouse, thinking how silly she was to have
trekked all the way out here after him—and for
what? She'd lost him. There was no sign of
Stefan. Yet she couldn't let it go. She'd seen him
come in here, he had to be somewhere near, and
she wanted to know why he was in the graveyard.

The large cemetery was quiet and peaceful.
The hot summer sun shone on white and gray
marble stones, the well-kept grass that covered
the buried dead. Emily didn't like cemeteries. As
a child, she had played hide-and-seek in a cemetery once, at dusk. It had been a frightening
experience to which her imagination had added
more scares than existed. Ever since then she'd
felt uncomfortable and wary inside a graveyard.
This cemetery was predominantly Jewish, she
noticed as she looked over the hills of marble

monuments and saw the Star of David rising over many against the blue sky.

A crippled man with a club foot came out of the gatehouse.

"You for Rabinowitz?" he asked.

"No," Emily said.

"Rabinowitz is over there." He pointed to a small group of mourners gathered around an open grave some distance away.

"I'm not for Rabinowitz," she repeated.

"Why didn't you say so?" he snapped, irritated. He went back into the gatehouse and banged the door shut.

Perhaps Stefan had joined the funeral, she thought as she walked over to the edge of the small crowd. She searched the sad faces but Stefan was not among them. Tall spires of cypress trees, bushy oak, and elm stood in groups at various parts of the cemetery, beautiful and solemn. She could smell the freshly cut grass.

And then she saw him. He stood some distance away by a huge tombstone, copying something down in a small notebook.

"It's very nice of you to come."

Emily started. A man had separated himself from the group and had come up beside Emily. "Thank you," Emily said, not knowing quite what else to say. She wanted to keep the protection of the crowd around her so she could watch Stefan unnoticed. She didn't want to lose him again.

"Are you from the office?" the man asked. His pale blue eyes were moist.

"No," said Emily nervously. Stefan had finished and was moving away, deeper into the sprawling cemetery.

"She was such a fine, compassionate woman," the man said, his chin trembling. Quite suddenly he burst into tears.

"Yes, yes, she was," Emily heard herself saying, touched by the man's grief but desperate to keep Stefan in view. "I'm sorry but I have to leave," she whispered to him. His shoulders were shaking with his quiet sobs. He didn't appear to hear her.

Stefan had disappeared.

Emily walked swiftly over to the spot where she'd seen Stefan writing in his notebook. It was a freshly dug grave. The grave marker said JESSE SACKADORF 1912–1951. She glanced at it, then strode on. Where had Stefan gone?

He reappeared moving farther away from her, a frail boy among the towering tombstones. She followed, skirting the graves. He was leading her away from the little pocket of mourners. She lost him again. *This is demented,* she thought, walking past a marble gravestone twice her height. Involuntarily, she shuddered, remembering her fear as a child when she'd been all alone in the Connecticut cemetery. She'd lost Jeff then, too, but he'd merely been hiding from her. How ironic, she thought, that ten years later Jeff was lying in one of the plots they'd chased over.

Stefan was nowhere around, but still she pressed on, stopping to look around, then moving on in the direction she'd last seen him take. She could see the elevated train and a corner of the station in the distance. She'd covered a wide semicircle; the cemetery entrance would be somewhere past a stand of cypress trees on her right. She walked past a family plot behind the cypress trees.

Suddenly, a hand shot out and grabbed her tightly by the wrist.

"She is wrong, your Dickinson," Stefan said in a rush. His face looked blank.

Emily, frightened, tried to pull her hand away, but he held her fast with much more strength than she would have imagined he could muster.

"She has poem, you know such poem? 'The heart seeks pleasure first.'" His large eyes stared at her, unblinking.

"Let me go!" She could feel her heart beating fast. She tried to pry his long fingers away from her wrist.

"You know this?" Stefan insisted, shaking her. He was looking at her with as little expression as a sleepwalker. She nodded, so frightened that she was unable to speak. He prompted her. "'The heart seeks pleasure first,'" he repeated.

Emily swallowed and finished the line. "'And then escape from pain. And then—'"

"She is wrong. First comes pain," Stefan said. His words chilled her. She looked around for an escape but there was none. They were completely alone by the cypress trees. "Exquisite pain so bright and keen the body soars. . . ." He seized her other wrist with fingers like claws. "Why do you follow me?" he hissed at her.

His grip was excruciating. "I wasn't—I mean, I—"

"Are you from government?" he demanded.

"The government?" she said, startled. "No, I—"

"What do want from me?" he demanded again, tightening his grip on her wrist.

Emily struggled against him. She began moaning. "I don't know . . . I'm not sure of anything," Emily said truthfully. "Please! You're hurting me! When I saw you with Salwen—"

His grip on her wrist was a vise. "There was no Salwen," he said through his teeth.

Grabbing at straws, she cried desperately, "I can help you!"

He hadn't expected to hear that. He loosened his grip on her, but not enough for her to escape. Her wrists throbbed.

"Why you think I need help?" he demanded.

"Because you're afraid."

"Of what?" he said faintly, looking even more alert.

"Of something. Someone," she replied, following her hunch. In her simple and honest way she said, "I know what that's like. Being afraid. You feel so alone!"

They stood together behind the huge trees staring at each other nakedly. She thought Stefan looked like an animal caught in a trap. He released her arm suddenly.

"Thank you." She rubbed her wrists and shook

the tears of pain out of her eyes. "I followed you because you lied to me. I know what Salwen looks like, and I saw him—"

"You are friend of Salwen?" asked Stefan, panicked.

"No." She was still being honest.

"How do I know that?" he asked, extremely wary of her.

"Well, you're the one who's lying, not me. And you're acting suspicious. The first thing you asked—was I from the government? Are you here illegally?" Stefan drew back as though she'd hit him. Emily hastened to reassure him. "Don't worry," she said, "I won't tell anyone. Maybe I can help you."

"You know nothing of me," he whispered. "Why should you help a stranger, a foreigner?"

Emily took a few steps toward him. She wanted to get out from behind the cypress trees. "Maybe because you look like you expect everyone to hurt you," she said, moving around the trees and into the open. She could see the gate of the cemetery now, and the elevated station rising ahead.

Stefan backed away. "How could you help?"

"I know lawyers. They specialize in problems like yours. I'll give you a few names."

She took a pen and a piece of paper from her purse and began to write, forming the letters with difficulty. Red welts were rising on her wrists.

"They're all in the phone book," she said. "If you need a place to stay, they'll find you one. You know my name . . . I'll put down my phone number, too, in case you need it."

She pressed the paper into his hand, but he was looking past her, over her shoulder. Emily had never seen the color drain from anyone's face before, but that's what was happening to Stefan. He was terrified. Feeling her heart stop, she turned.

On the elevated subway platform, across the street from the cemetery, a man was leaning against the railing. He was looking directly down at them, his face lazy and composed, a cigarette dangling from his fingers. Emily didn't sense anything frightening about the man, but Stefan was undone.

"Who is that?" she asked.

"McKay," he breathed. "What have you done to me?" Stefan cried out in anguish. He pushed her aside and ran off.

His fear was so thick she thought she could smell it in the air around her. A second later, he disappeared among the tombstones. She looked back at the station. McKay was gone.

The subway was crowded as Emily headed back to Manhattan—standing room only. In the tunnel, the train sat in its dark tube under the river like an obstruction. The sweat rolled off her, soaking the back of her dress. The car was packed, people as cattle; they figeted, anxious at the delay, irritated in the heat, a bone of fear plucking at those who always looked for disaster. The image of the dark tracks lacing under hundreds of feet of water stirred her. Every New Yorker knew what a submarine hiding from the enemy was like.

When she finally climbed the steps to her apartment, Emily leaned against the door. She felt scrungy and sticky. The look on Stefan's face when he saw McKay, the man with the lazy, cruel smile, stayed with her. What was she getting herself into, she wondered.

Liberty mewed and sniffed at her delicately, then marched away, offended. Emily went to the front windows and looked out. People were walking by the building below, but she couldn't recognize any of them from the tops of their heads; she checked the parked cars but didn't see anyone sitting in them. She also didn't see anyone lounging around in doorways. Had anyone followed her? She'd never know. Vertigo seized her; sometimes even this second-story height was too much for her. She lowered the venetian blinds and shut them with a snap.

Don't get excited, she told herself. But it was more than the height—it was a new fear that swept over her. Stefan had been very frightened; in fact, he'd been terrorized. That was real, that wasn't some game. Metzger's suicide was real, too. She filled a teakettle, set it on the stove, and lit the gas burner. But why was Stefan so frightened, and what did Salwen have to do with it? She thought about Stefan. He was appealing; perhaps it was the gentleness that lay beneath his fear. And he was just a boy. *I better call Alan,* she thought. She was being drawn into an odd and menacing web—it was like feeling her way along dark walls. She didn't know what was at the end of the corridor.

Liberty meowed, demanding a dinner that was very slow in coming. The doorbell rang. Emily stiffened. In a way that surprised her, she didn't want to answer it. Who would it be? What did they want? It rang again, demanding.

"Who is it?" Emily said to the door.

"Federal Bureau of Investigation."

"I have nothing to say to you," Emily replied tightly.

"We've got a search warrant," the man said threateningly.

"Slip it under the door," she said. She looked at the floor as a paper slid across the threshold. She picked it up and read it. It was a search warrant, and it had *official* written all over it.

Slowly she opened the door. The same two FBI agents who had been accosting her for months, and who'd been at Miss Venable's stood in front of her.

Hackett, the older man, was wearing his formal, tight, FBI manner. He said, "Your organization has failed to register under the Subversive Activities Control Act after being placed on the attorney general's subversive activities list. The act gives us the legal right therefore to search your place of residence for your membership records."

"That's incredible," Emily said. "You can just come into people's homes and—" She stopped talking, trying to find a more objective manner. Losing her temper wouldn't help anything. "I'm calling my lawyer," she stated.

"We're coming in, Miss Crane," said Hackett. "If you resist, that's a felony. You want that?"

She hesitated. "Of course I don't want a felony," she said. She turned, leaving the door open, and went to the phone.

They came in. Cochran closed the door behind him. Emily watched them as they split apart, Cochran going into the bedroom, Hackett into the kitchen. *They're practiced at this*, she thought, lifting the phone and dialing.

Alan's secretary, Peggy, answered. Emily remembered her as a chubby girl from the Bronx with great-looking eyes.

"Mr. Dworkin, please," Emily said, trying to keep her voice calm. She could hear cupboards and drawers being opened.

"I'm sorry," said Peggy. She was chewing gum. Emily remembered her saying once that it was "good for the gums, if you get me."

"When will he be back?" Emily asked.

"Who's calling?" asked Peg.

When Emily told her, Peg said that she didn't know when he'd be back, that he'd gone out.

"Let's find him," Emily said testily, hearing more drawers being opened in the bedroom. Peggy told her that she didn't know where they'd gone. Emily began to hear her voice rising as she said, "Well, ask him, please, to call me. As soon as he comes in. It's very important."

She hung up, frustrated. She felt like crying. Hackett came back into the living room and methodically began to search it. He was very professional, very detached; he ignored her. Liberty had been hiding under the sofa. She darted out and raced into the bedroom, giving Hackett a wide berth. Emily felt violated, helpless in her own home. It was a completely new and degrading feeling.

As he picked up a little ceramic horse her father had given her as a child, she said, "These are my things. They aren't open for inspection." She couldn't keep her voice from trembling. "Do you think I keep the membership rolls in that horse?" She felt victimized and outraged at the same time.

She went into the bedroom. Cochran was lifting a box off a closet shelf. "That's a quilt," she said. Like Hackett, he was neat, professional, and quick. He glanced at her, peeked into the box, then replaced it. The bedroom looked undisturbed. He'd put everything back exactly the way it was.

Liberty came out from behind a chair, went over and sniffed his shoes. "Liberty, come here," Emily said, but the cat paid no attention to her. Instead, she put her head on Cochran's shoe and meowed. He looked down.

"Nice puss," he said, bending to pet her. He chucked the cat under the chin, then scratched behind its ears. "I like cats, and you know it, don'tcha?" he said to her.

Emily made a face. Of all the betrayals this was surely the most humiliating—Liberty groveling at the FBI's shoes.

"Do you want to examine my lingerie?" she asked suddenly, marching over to her bureau and pulling open a drawer. "I suppose that's what really makes your job interesting!"

"I've already checked your—one of the dressers," he said quietly. He glanced at her, then his eyes settled on some framed photos of her friends, and one of her brother beside her bed. He went over to them.

"Don't touch those," Emily warned him. "I don't keep files in my photographs, and I don't want your hands on my pictures." She felt as if she'd club him with the umbrella if he did. Cochran halted, and veered away to a small three-drawer dresser on the other side of the room. Liberty followed him.

He opened the first drawer and felt around among her nightgowns. She watched him scornfully.

"Don't you have anything better to do? Not enough kidnappers around? Or counterfeiters?" she asked sarcastically.

Cochran didn't look at her. He opened the second drawer. "The Treasury Department."

"What?" she demanded, glad she had found her anger. "You're muttering."

"The Treasury Department handles counterfeiters," he said in a louder voice.

"I stand corrected." She watched him open the last drawer, which held her pedal-pushers. "What do you handle besides what doesn't belong to you?"

Suddenly he turned on her, a look of weary exasperation in his eyes. "Look. I don't get a kick out of this. I don't get a kick out of you, either. You and your friends. You don't like this country, why don't you—"

"—go back where we came from?" Emily said,

finishing his thought. "What a tiresome old cliché."

"You don't know how lucky you are," he said, gazing at her. "Some other places—"

"I'm not *in* some other places. I'm here, where I was born," she said. The nerve of this guy. He reached down again and ran a hand along Liberty's back. She noticed that Cochran moved with a kind of easy grace and it made her even more angry at him. "And where do you get off, telling me how lucky I am?"

"Have you ever had to live like those people you're always sticking up for? Did you ever go without a meal in your whole life?" he demanded. "Did anyone ever shoot at you, lady? Do you know what you are? You're a privileged—" Cochran stopped. He didn't want to go any further with it.

Emily walked over to him across the room that he had violated and smudged. This room would never be hers again in the same way. "Say it," she said in a dangerously sweet voice. "Go on, say it. I'm a privileged—what?" She hated him. She would never have believed that she could truly loathe another human being as she did right now.

Cochran saw her hatred. He slammed the drawer shut.

"If that's broken, you'll pay for it!" she said.

"You finished?" Hackett asked, coming into the room. Emily and Cochran were glaring at each other. Liberty was lying on her back exposing her belly at Cochran's feet.

"Damn right," Cochran said.

At the front door, Hackett turned and smirked at her.

"Be seeing you, Miss Crane."

Emily slammed the door after them and double-locked it. She was still in a rage. Liberty meowed. Emily turned on her. "And you—" she said. "I thought you had better taste!"

Chapter 6

Outside Emily's apartment on West Eighty-fourth Street, Hackett started the motor of the nondescript, gray car the FBI supplied to its agents. "How long have you been with the Bureau, Mike?" Hackett asked, pulling the car out and heading east to Broadway.

"Since law school. Why?" He was still angry. He'd never met anyone who could get under his skin as fast as that Emily Crane.

"Out west, right?" asked Hackett. "A college in one of those farm states?"

"Yeah, Kansas. One of those farm states where the wheat blows in the wind." Cochran thought briefly of the wide Kansas spaces where the golden wheat danced against the deep blue sky.

"They have girls out there?" Hackett asked.

"Come on, Sid," said Cochran. "What are you getting at?"

"Good-looking girls with blond hair?" he pressed. "You've seen them? You've heard what they can do to you?"

Cochran faced the older man. "She got me mad. That's all it was." He couldn't keep the defensive note out of his voice and it made him even more angry.

"This is a job," Hackett said seriously. "You don't get mad, you don't get personal—even if you come from the sticks where everybody says hello."

The light changed, and Hackett edged the car into the heavy traffic on Broadway, heading south. Cochran ran a hand over his jaw. The car hit a deep pothole and bounced them both in the air.

"I don't like this city," Cochran said. He leaned back against the seat and thought of the wheatfields again, of the sweet air, of the little blue flowers that grew at the sides of the straight, timeless road cutting east to west.

Emily was repositioning what Cochran and Hackett had touched, trying to put her own imprint back on her belongings. She was still mad, primarily at the young one, Cochran. The phone rang and she leaped to it.

"Alan!" she cried as a wave of relief rolled over her. "Listen, the FBI was here! With a search warrant. They went through the whole apartment." She felt the tears bunching behind her eyes. Her throat constricted painfully. "I tried to reach you, but—"

"Emily Crane?" It wasn't Alan at all.

"Who is this?" she said, swallowing.

"You are Emily Crane who reads Dickinson?" the light voice asked.

She was talking to Stefan! "Oh, yes . . . yes," she said. "I thought you were somebody else." She reached into her pocket and pulled out a handkerchief.

"You think still you can help me?" he asked. His voice was very low and she had to strain to hear him. She daubed her hanky at her eyes.

"I can try," she said, honestly.

"I would like to meet again with you."

"Yes. Well, I don't think we should meet here." And then a thought occurred to her. "I'll tell you where. Sheridan Square at the bookstore. You can't miss it, it's quite large and they sell secondhand books."

"It is safe?" Stefan asked, concerned.

"Oh, yes. There'll be people all around," Emily assured him.

"You can be there nine o'clock tonight?"

"Yes, I'll be there," she said.

"I see you at bookstore. Nine o'clock."

The line went dead. She stared at the receiver. Then she called Alan again.

"Oh, Alan, I'm so glad I reached you. The goddamned FBI was here with a warrant. And I've—well, there's someone I want you to meet. He needs advice." Quickly, Emily told him about meeting Stefan and his possible connection to Salwen.

"Emily, I know you want revenge for what Salwen and the committee is doing to you and—"

"Alan, no! Listen, I've got more questions than answers about Stefan, but I think he was a child in the concentration camps."

"Emily, getting involved like this is dumb of you, but if you want me to see him, I will."

"Oh, thank you, Alan. I'll explain everything when I see you." She hung up, still thinking about Stefan. If he had been a victim of the camps, why would he be in the States illegally? There were many refugees from the camps here —legally. Could he have worked in the camps, could that be it? Was he German? She gave up.

"I am giving you this," she said, putting the cat food down in Liberty's dish, "even though you made a perfect fool of yourself with the FBI tonight." Liberty dug in without a shred of visible guilt.

The bookstore on Sheridan Square in the Village was lit up brilliantly. Crowds of people flowed one way and another, going out to dinner, to the theater, chasing in and out of their apartments for the forgotten quart of milk or to pick up a newspaper. It was summer in the Village. As Emily had predicted, the bookstore was a very public place.

When Emily arrived shortly before nine that night, the proprietor, a plump man with a bushy black mustache, sat behind the cash register, reading and keeping an eye on the door. A dozen or so people were browsing in the store, but Stefan was not among them. She walked between the high rows of shelves, stacked with books of all description, past History and Travel, looking for him. It was five after nine. She began to worry as she moved into Music, and spotted a book she'd once wanted on Lizst. She plucked it out of the shelf and opened it.

"Are you alone?" It was Stefan. He was on the other side of the shelving at the end of the last row, hidden between the stacks. She put the book down and went around to his side.

"Yes, of course," she whispered. "Are you all right?" His dark eyes looked wild; his hair was messed up, and the collar of his jacket was half up and half down.

"I am in a very bad position," he hissed. His eyes were never still. He looked down the row of shelves, to the right and left, then back at her again. "Bad things are happening in that house. I wish not to be part anymore."

"The house on Carroll Street?" she asked. He nodded, his eyes combing the bookstore. "Shouldn't you go to the police?"

"No! No, of no use." He rejected that suggestion out of hand. He was clearly very frightened. "You say you can help."

"Well, I called one of those lawyers I mentioned. He's waiting for us at his house." Emily tried to sound calm, as Alan had instructed her, but it was very difficult with Stefan.

"He is a good man, this lawyer? You trust him?" Stefan asked, wanting to be sure, but not believing that any safety would ever be his.

"Absolutely."

"Very well," he sighed. He looked like he was going to cry.

She reached out. "Wait," she said, and straightened his collar. "There." He looked at her. She could see the tears in his eyes. They started for the front door.

"We can get a cab across the street," Emily said as they passed the owner of the store, still absorbed in his book.

As Emily pulled open the front door and gestured to Stefan to follow her, two large men on the other side blocked the way.

"Excuse me," Emily said, trying to get past them.

"Okay, sonny, let's go," one of them said to Stefan. He had a gravelly voice and a square face.

Stefan whirled around, but the other man seized him.

"Take your hands off him!" Emily demanded shrilly.

The first man flashed a badge at her and growled, "Immigration. He's an illegal alien."

Stefan was struggling wildly, his arms flailing. "They are not Immigration!" he screamed at Emily.

The other people in the store were drawn to the front by the noise. They watched curiously. The owner threw down his book, slid off his stool by the cash register, and rolled over to them.

"What's going on?" he demanded. The first man showed him his badge and said something to him quietly. Emily saw the owner nod and back away.

"You can't do this!" cried Emily to the men, seeing that the owner wasn't going to help.

"Emily!" Stefan screamed, anguished. He was still struggling, but the beefy second man had him firmly in hand. He was not going to get away. "Take it easy, son," the large man said. "Nobody's going to hurt you."

Emily didn't know what to do or who to believe, but the terror in Stefan's eyes and voice was very real to her. The first man now took hold of Stefan's left arm, and together the men began skating him back to the front door. Emily kept pace with them.

"Where are you taking him?" she asked.

"Downtown," the first man said.

"No! Emily! Help me!" Stefan cried out.

"Don't worry, Stefan, I'll get the lawyer!" Emily said.

"They are not from Immigration!" Stefan pleaded with her. "Believe me!"

"Quiet, son." The second man applied more pressure on Stefan's arm, pulling it back and twisting it up.

"Please . . . help me," Stefan moaned, his knees buckling. The men lifted him, dragging him toward the door.

"I'll go with you," she said. "I'll call the lawyer from their office. They can't keep you from having a lawyer." All the people in the store were bunched behind her, watching quietly and whispering.

"Sorry, Miss Crane," the first man said. "You can't do that. Regulations."

In that second, before she realized what had triggered it, a constellation of images pelted her—the look in the man's pale eyes, the lock he had on the frail Stefan, the combative way he was reaching for the handle of the front door.

She suddenly knew that Stefan was right: they were not from Immigration.

"How do you know my name?" she demanded sharply.

The second man instantly realized they had made a mistake. His pale eyes slipped toward his companion, who was hustling Stefan along roughly. The first man had the door open and was trying to pull Stefan through it when Emily grabbed Stefan and, with all her strength, yanked him violently out of their grasp.

"Run!" Emily screamed to Stefan. "Run!"

He dashed backward into the store and around a large table stacked high with secondhand sale books. The men recovered clumsily and started after him, but Stefan swept the stack of books into their path. They stumbled, and one man went down. As they struggled to get to their feet, Stefan did an about-face, leaped a stack of books, and shot out the door. Emily was right on his heels.

"Hey!" yelled the bookstore owner.

It only took the men a moment to kick the books aside but it was just the moment Stefan and Emily needed. Cursing, the men bounded out of the bookstore. Emily and Stefan were racing through the crowds, narrowly missing those in their path. Out of breath, Emily caught up with Stefan.

"Down here!" she panted. They cut down an alley cluttered with garbage and boxes. Stefan ran without grace but he was speedy and light on his feet. In his terror and confusion, he collided with a large carton and fell, but he quickly picked himself up. They rushed out of the alley, down another street, into another alley. Emily was gasping for breath and commanding her legs to obey her. "This way!" she yelled at Stefan. They burst out of the second alley and into a side street that Emily didn't recognize. The two large men were nowhere in sight.

"Wait, wait," Emily whispered. She leaned against a wall, holding her chest. He stopped beside her, breathing hoarsely.

Down the street, Emily saw a group of people standing around under a marquee, smoking and chatting. It was intermission at an off-Broadway theater, the Cherry Lane. "C'mon," panted Emily. She swept a hand over her hair, trying to smooth it down. They slowly walked up to the crowd and tried to look as if they belonged, standing on the fringes of it, getting their breath under control.

"Typical," said a man smoking a pipe. "The second act's a disaster. When are playwrights going to learn—"

"What *do* you *mean*?" said his companion, a short, dark-haired woman in a checked skirt. "The second act is a brilliant lead-in to the dénouement. It's all in the character of Priscilla."

"No, no," the man said, in a fatherly fashion, puffing on his pipe. "Priscilla is not the key here at all! It's David's play."

Emily leaned against the brick wall of the theater.

"Stefan," she said, "who were those guys?"

He was slicking down his hair and buttoning his jacket. "They are Matilde's men," he whispered. "I had no permission to go out tonight. They know I am trying to escape."

The intermission bell rang and the audience started to file back into the theater. "But from what?" Emily asked Stefan. "What's going on?"

He shook his head. "Shhh," he cautioned. As the crowd thinned out, they were conspicuous and exposed as interlopers. Emily glanced around and saw, to her horror, that the two men had appeared far down the street. But they still hadn't spotted Emily and Stefan; they were looking in every doorway, making their sweep up the street.

"Into the theater," she said to Stefan. "We're part of the audience now. And let's just pray someone didn't like the play and left." She took his arm and guided him into the theater.

This is all so ordinary, she thought, watching the audience settle into their seats, *and we're being chased by God knows who—*

"Stefan, what's going on?" she hissed.

"It is a cover—a deceit—" He hunted for words, whispering next to her ear.

"A cover-up?"

He nodded. "The assistants Dr. Teperson—"

He stopped talking. Most of the audience had seated themselves. Once again Emily and Stefan were exposed, outside the safety of a crowd. An usher glanced at them, then closed the doors. The lights began to dim. Stefan spotted two empty seats on the left side. They settled into them as the curtain rose.

"Priscilla," said an actor, "was there a fight in the rose garden?"

"A disreputable boor!" snapped an actress in a stylish black dress. "They ruined my afternoon in the rose garden."

Emily was checking out the exits. She glanced at the back of the house. *Damn*, she thought, feeling a spasm of fear shoot through her. The two men were standing against the back wall, systematically surveying the audience. She nudged Stefan and hunched down in her seat.

"But didn't they know there are no roses now?" David said darkly as Priscilla wrestled with a drink caddy.

"I think you're in our seats," hissed a voice next to Emily's ear. She looked up and was facing the dim outline of the boring man with the pipe. She could smell his pipe tobacco on his breath.

"I don't think we are," Emily bluffed. She could feel the eyes of the watching men at the back being drawn to this knot of obtrusive action in the audience.

"Well, you certainly are!" the man said more loudly, puffing pipe tobacco at Emily. She glanced back. The men were staring at them. In a moment, they'd be coming down the aisle.

"I thought you didn't like this play," Emily said to the startled man. She sprang out of her seat. Stefan leaped from his into the aisle, pushing the man and his date aside. The two men from the bookstore broke into a trot, starting down the aisle—bulky, heavy shapes, coming toward them.

"Back that way," Emily hissed, urging Stefan toward the side aisle and a door labeled EXIT in red. They pushed it open and flew through it. They were backstage.

"Where's the door?" asked Stefan. "We have to get out!"

"I don't know!"

"Hey, you can't come in here." It was the stage manager.

"We just want to get out, that's all," said Emily. "Please . . . how do we get out?"

An actor in a top hat and a clown's outfit shushed them.

"Next time use the front door, lady," said the stage manager, pointing to the stage door.

"Thanks," Emily hissed as they hurried to the door. She grabbed Stefan's hand, pushed the door open, and stood against it as he tumbled forward. He was halfway through it when he froze.

The man who'd so frightened Stefan at the cemetery stood in the alley just outside the door.

"McKay!" Stefan breathed. He reached back involuntarily, his hand finding Emily's shoulder just as she saw the knife blade glitter in the light over the stage door.

Emily could feel a scream forming in her throat, but she was too terrified to push it out. Horrified, she watched McKay raise the knife in a short practiced arc, catching Stefan just under his rib cage. McKay twisted the knife, then abruptly withdrew it, stepping back. Stefan staggered, making a sound somewhere between a squeal and a groan, and dropped to his knees, clutching his stomach. He fell forward, hitting his forehead hollowly on the pavement. He crumpled onto his side, his arms still gripping the massively bleeding wound. The whole thing had only taken a few seconds.

Emily knelt beside Stefan as McKay's footsteps receded down the alley in quick clicks. He was gone. Stefan's mouth was moving. She bent down; blood spattered against her cheek. His big eyes looked at her, saw her, then stopped seeing her as blood ballooned out of his mouth. At last Emily found her voice, and she screamed.

Chapter 7

Lieutenant Martin Sloan had been raised in New York. In his youth—a time he could barely remember from the distance of middle age and twenty years on the force—he'd once toyed with the idea of being an actor. He was a deep-chested man with a robust voice and an animated, lively face. He was also tough; if pressed, he could be mean.

Sloan was talking on the stage manager's telephone backstage at the theater, eyeing the young, pretty, and distressed woman who'd been with the murdered man. She was sitting off to one side, staring vacantly ahead, still in shock. Her blond hair fell over half her face; she held her hands tightly knotted in her lap. Sloan had sent the audience home, but the stage and alley were still crowded with policemen, detectives, men from forensics, a handful of witnesses—stage manager, a guy in a clown suit—and a few curious onlookers from the cast. Conversations were muted.

Sloan hung up the telephone receiver and walked across to Emily.

"Nothing," he said heavily to Emily. "Nobody knows who he is. Nobody knows where he lived. No ID on him. Fingerprints, clothes . . . zero. Nothing. He didn't exist."

"I told you before," Emily said dully. "Go to that house."

"Look, Miss Crane, we ran a check on you. You're in a little bit of trouble yourself." He hitched his trousers up. "You want my advice? Don't look for more." Sloan thought he sounded reasonable and patient.

"The boy was in trouble," Emily said. She was repeating herself. She had no idea how long she'd been backstage sitting on this crate. "He was trying to get away."

"What trouble? Who was he trying to get away from?" Sloan asked. "Who murdered him? A fact or two, Miss Crane, would be more than helpful."

"Ask Samuel Salwen" was all Emily could tell him.

"Why?" he asked.

"I saw him with the boy," she said.

"You *think* you saw him," Sloan replied, correcting her.

"I know I did!" Emily shook her hair back and looked up at him. She was adamant.

"It's just your say-so, Miss Crane," Sloan sighed.

"Why should I lie?" she asked.

Sloan shrugged, and from a deep well of cynicism, filled regularly over the years, he said, "Everybody lies."

"I don't. Go back to that house. Talk to Salwen. That's all I can tell you," she said, sick at heart over the whole business. "I don't know what's going on, but whatever it is, it's—terrible."

"Miss Crane," Sloan said, selecting a new tack. "I like being a cop. That might surprise you. I also want to stay a cop. So I don't bother important people unless I got something to bother them about. Do you read me?"

A detective in a wrinkled gray suit and a fedora broke away from the knot of police by the stage door, strode across to Sloan, and whispered in his ear. Sloan looked out over the theater and Emily followed his gaze. Mike Cochran was standing at the rear of the seats with another detective.

"Okay, you can go," Sloan said to Emily.

"Did you have to get permission from the FBI?" she asked.

Sloan narrowed his eyes. "Don't crowd your luck. We could book you as a material witness." Exhausted, she got off the crate. "Wait a minute. You know any of these names?" Sloan asked her. He flipped open his notebook and read from it. "Samuel Hurwitz. David Bistrong. Jesse Sackadorf." He looked up at her suddenly alert. "They mean anything to you? The kid had them in his pocket." he said.

Emily kept her face blank. Bistrong and Hurwitz didn't mean anything, but Sackadorf was the name on the gravestone yesterday. She met his eyes and shook her head. Sloan was right, she thought. Everyone lies.

"Good night, Miss Crane," Sloan said with finality.

He turned to the clown in the top hat who was waiting nearby. Emily went down the little steps and into the side aisle of the theater. Cochran was waiting for her in the lobby.

"Miss Crane," he said, taking off his hat. "I'm sorry about the boy."

She walked past him. "Are you still following me?" she asked.

"Can I give you a lift?" he asked. She kept on walking until she reached the street. "It's tough getting a cab this time of night," Cochran tried again, following her.

She looked up and down the dark street. There were no cabs. Emily started walking west, heading for Sixth Avenue. Cochran kept up with her. He had not been able to get her out of his mind since they'd searched her apartment. It was the look of violation in her eyes that had stayed with him.

After a block she stopped and faced him. "Have you got a warrant for this?" she demanded.

"It's just late, that's all," Cochran said, still holding his hat. He wondered what Hackett would think if he knew his partner was trying to make peace with a suspect.

"That's all?" Emily cried, outraged. "Is *that* what you said, 'That's all!'" Her rage and her fear at what had happened flew out of her. Her face twisted and she raised her fists. "Nobody even knows his name! He didn't exist!" she sputtered.

"There are a lot of people like that," he said heavily and unhappily.

"No! That's where you're wrong!" she cried. "There was just *one* of him, *that's* all. Like one of you and one of me. But I'm the one who saw him die. I bet that's nothing new to you, but I never saw anyone die before. You know how long it took him? Maybe a minute. One minute he's alive and the next minute he's lying in a bloody heap in an alley. Why?" She looked up at him and then looked away. "Why am I telling you this?" She sounded, and she felt, so tired she could drop to the pavement. "I don't believe I'm having this conversation. You—you sneak and spy on people. . . . I'm a respectable person! This is *my* country, I am a good citizen! I want a world where people die in bed!" She stepped back from him, and her voice started to tremble. She felt utterly alone. "I am so scared. But I'm not stopping. I'm going to get to the reasons for why that boy was killed. And you can't scare me off. I will fight you for what I believe. And I believe there can be justice. Not order—I despise order. Justice! And I'm going to get it! Do you hear that?"

She stalked off into the night, disappearing into the shadows on Minetta Lane. Mike Cochran stared after her. She was a handful.

Emily sat in her bathtub trying to soak away her fear. Had there ever been another time in her life when she had felt as unsafe or in physical danger? She didn't think so.

When she had reached home that night, she had walked directly into the bathroom and turned the water on. She'd undressed, flinging the clothes that had witnessed death away from her in a heap on the floor. Liberty sat on her bed, watching quietly. The tub was filling, but very slowly. She grabbed her robe, tied it tightly around her narrow waist, and went back into the living room. She sat down at the little maplewood desk and wrote down the names Lieutenant Sloan had asked her about: Hurwitz, Bistrong, Sackadorf. She stared at them and then added a fourth name: Teperson. The man at the window who spoke German.

The telephone rang. It was her mother. She was coming into town soon and wanted to have lunch. "You don't sound like yourself, dear," said Mrs. Crane. Emily sighed.

"I'll see you at lunch, Mother."

Now Emily was relaxing into the hot water in the tub. She closed her eyes. It was so hard to believe that Stefan was dead. But another part of her—a more vulnerable and defenseless part of her—believed it utterly. What was it he had known that had frightened him so, and frightened other people to the point of killing him so he would not tell? She didn't feel up to finding out. She was too frightened herself. Automatically, unbidden, as she let her mind drift, she went through everything she'd done after she'd reached the harbor of her apartment. Had she

locked the front door? How about the windows?
They were always locked, weren't they? She
tried to force herself to relax but only became
more tense.

She heard a faint sound from the living room
and sat bolt upright in the tub. Silence. Had she
really heard it? Was she imagining it? Liberty
meowed. She reached over and pushed at the
bathroom door. It swung open slowly.

Salwen was sitting in a chair, looking at her.

"You don't mind? I was in the neighborhood,"
he said, amiably.

Emily shrank back into the tub, speechless
and frightened out of her wits. He had placed a
straight-backed chair from her kitchen directly
behind the bathroom door. The towel she'd been
resting her head against sank slowly into the
water.

"Normally, I would have called first," he went
on, crossing his legs, looking at his nails, "but
these are not normal times. I can close the door
if you want to get out." She made no move at all.
"No? No." He looked down at the cuff of his
handsome trousers and brushed off a cat hair.
"Tell me, do you like reading to that crazy old
lady?" he asked, looking sharply up at her. "It's
a job far beneath your capabilities. You're a
smart, intelligent young woman. You had a
promising future."

"What do you want?" Emily whispered jagged-
ly, aware that she had folded her arms over her
breasts but not remembering doing it.

"I'd like to help you," Salwen said, almost
musically.

114

"Why?" she asked. The horror of being at his mercy, naked, in the bathtub, was subsiding. This visit was only a warning, she was sure of it. She wanted to reach up for a towel and cover herself, but it would give him too much satisfaction.

Salwen was smiling and dimples appeared on his cheeks. "Y is a crooked letter," he said. "My mother used to say that to me when I asked too many questions." He stopped talking, uncrossed his legs, and put his elbows on his knees, leaning forward as if to speak to her confidentially. "Emily . . . may I call you Emily? You don't mind? The question is—what do you want? To get or not to get, that is the question. I'm concerned for your welfare."

"Like you were concerned about that boy's welfare?" she said bluntly.

Salwen's expression altered; his face looked sad and hurt. "I sought you out, Emily. I didn't have to come here, you know. You're not important enough to buy off."

"Then why try? Why *are* you here?"

"Nobody wants another mess," he replied evenly.

His words hung in the air. *He's really enjoying this,* Emily thought as she stared at him, fascinated. *My God, he's really dangerous.*

He held up a piece of paper. "You left this on your desk, Emily," he said. "Do you know these gentlemen?" Emily didn't answer. "Hurwitz, Sackadorf, Bistrong." He paused and sighed. "And Teperson." As punctuation he let the paper drift to the floor. "Now these men are really dangerous," he counseled her softly. "Don't stay too long in the hot tub." He flashed a smile and rose. "You could catch your death." He turned gracefully, smoothing the front of his beautifully tailored coat, and walked back into the living room. A moment later, she heard the front door open and close quietly.

Chapter 8

Marilyn put a bowl of Wheaties in front of Emily. Jerry sat in his high chair banging a spoon rhythmically against the edge of the table.

"Gene Krupa," Emily said, tilting her head at Jerry.

"Jerry!" Alan said sharply. The child, who was more baby than boy, arrested his spoon in midair and looked at him combatively. "I mean it." Alan looked to his wife, who was sitting down at the breakfast table for the first time since Emily arrived.

"You've had two big shocks," Marilyn said to Emily. She took the spoon out of Jerry's hand and replaced it with a paper napkin. "Sitting in on your bath—the idea!"

"It was a warning," Emily said to her Wheaties. She felt that Alan and Marilyn couldn't possibly understand. She felt trapped in a situation the way a train was trapped on its tracks.

"Now look here," Alan said, taking charge. "Don't go back to your apartment. Come and stay here. If he can get in so easily, it's not safe!"

"But I know I locked the door!" Emily said.

"You probably just think you did but it didn't catch," said Marilyn, watching Jerry shred the napkin.

"Marilyn, I locked it."

"Honey," Alan said, "there are all kinds of ways professionals can get in doors these days." He picked up a piece of toast and turned back to Emily. "I can't believe Salwen's run amuck. Why would he get involved with something like the boy's murder?" Alan mumbled. "He's just got too much to lose."

"You don't believe me," Emily said.

"Of course we believe you!" Alan cried a little too heartily.

"Let's not think about that now," said Marilyn briskly. "How do we protect Emily?" Jerry coughed. He was eating the napkin. "Oh, Jesus," she sighed, opening his mouth and digging around for the shredded paper.

Emily pushed her Wheaties away. "Look, all I want to know is what kind of aliens enter illegally. That's the key to this thing."

"Lots of groups. That isn't any key," Alan replied, crunching his toast. "Nazis, Nazi collaborators, communists, communist collaborators, communist spies, refugees who can't prove they weren't in any of those camps—all of those, any of those!"

"Stefan said his last name was Hudak," Emily said. "That's Polish."

"So he could be Polish," Alan said, grinning. "Believe me, Emily, he could be anything. He could have just taken that name. Didn't he tell you anything?" Emily shook her head. "Well, you've got to stop playing detective. I agree with you—you've been warned by Salwen. He's very powerful, and he's obviously got all the machinery of government on his side."

"Oh, Alan," Marilyn said, disgusted, "the government isn't interested in seeing Emily dead."

"I never said that!" he snapped. They were irritated with each other and worried about Emily. "I meant that Emily has been tainted since her appearance before the committee. She's not going to get a lot of sympathy or protection out of the police. What was it that detective said last night, that Sloan guy?"

"That I'm in trouble myself. Anyway, Sloan doesn't believe me about seeing Salwen at the house on Carroll Street. And he certainly wouldn't believe me that Salwen visited my bath last night." She felt so removed from Marilyn and Alan, from their cozy home that ran around the schedule of Alan's work and Jerry's nursery school and the groceries.

Jerry was picking up a fistful of damp Wheaties. Emily stared at the child lugubriously.

"Emily, don't go back to your apartment," Marilyn said. "Don't go to your job, don't do anything."

"Marilyn," said Alan in warning, watching Jerry drop wet Wheaties on the floor.

Marilyn turned. "Why don't *you* do something about Jerry for once?" she snapped at Alan.

Alan, angry, rose. "I'm going to work." He shouldered into his jacket. "You stay here, Emily."

Marilyn went out to the hall with him. Emily heard them whispering about Salwen. She knew they didn't believe her about Salwen's peculiar and sinister visit.

After Alan had left, Marilyn said, "You're just not going to do the sensible thing, are you?"

Emily smiled a little. "I can't just let everything drop," she said quietly. "I saw Stefan die. You don't know how horrible that is. And I feel guilty about it. He came to me for help, and I—"

"You couldn't have known some nut would kill him!"

"'Some nut' didn't kill him. McKay killed him."

"For God's sake, Emily, don't be a fool! Why are you doing this?" Marilyn asked, exasperated.

Emily pushed a strand of hair away from her face and leaned back in her chair with a sigh. "I can't just back away. That's what so many people are doing today—the hearings, the firings, the loyalty oaths, the investigations, the FBI following people and searching their apartments . . ." She leaned forward intensely. "I can't do it, Marilyn! That house in back of Miss Venable's, there's something going on there, something illicit that killed the boy, and I'm just not going to back away. Do you realize that I'm the only person who knows that Salwen was there with Stefan?"

"All the more reason to drop it," Marilyn said grimly. Jerry put his fist into his milky bowl of

Wheaties and let out an ear-piercing cry of delight.

Miss Venable's chair was empty when Emily reported for work that morning. Alarmed, ready to believe anything after the events of last night, she turned to Alma.

"Miss Venable will be down presently," Alma said in her nasal Bronx voice. "Have some tea." Emily took a cup back to the shrouded living room and sipped it, thinking about Salwen and his oily, confident, upper-class manner. She felt in jeopardy whenever he was around. But really, what could she do about any of this? Lieutenant Sloan wasn't going to muddy the waters by "disturbing important people," and Salwen was definitely one of those.

"Are you unwell, Miss Crane?" Miss Venable had glided silently into the room and caught Emily deep in thought.

"I'm fine," Emily lied. "I just haven't been sleeping too well."

"Your health is a matter of concern to me," Miss Venable said, sitting in her wing chair and adjusting her brilliant turquoise dress. She touched the garnet and pearl brooch fastened at the neck of the gown, and pulled a black shawl around her shoulders.

"Thank you," Emily replied.

"You read with expression. Many people do not. Especially young people. They prefer pictures," Miss Venable said with a note of disapproval in her voice. "They do not realize that one word is worth a thousand pictures. The Chinese are quite mistaken on that score. A picture shows only what is there. A word can summon up a universe." She paused. "I disapprove of snooping, Miss Crane," Miss Venable finished abruptly.

Emily was taken aback. "I beg your pardon?" she said.

"You show an unseemly interest in that house across the garden," Miss Venable said.

"I'm sorry. I didn't mean—" Emily began to apologize.

"What one means is irrelevant. What matters is what one does." Miss Venable's sharp, pale eyes scanned Emily. "Just what is the nature of your interest?"

Emily looked boldly back at the old lady and decided to confide in her. Miss Venable was no fool. "I think that house is connected with something terrible." *In for a penny, in for a pound,* she thought.

"Does it concern you?" Miss Venable asked.

"Not exactly, but—"

"Then you have no reason to pry," Miss Venable said sternly.

Emily waited for another token from the East of Miss Venable's wisdom, or another strong opinion—even an ultimatum—but Miss Venable had closed her eyes. Emily picked up the new book. It was called *The Countess from Wyman Hall.* The cover displayed a beautiful raven-haired woman, costumed in the 1820s Empire period, and behind her a huge Tudoresque mansion.

"I do not know who lives in that house nor do I

care," Miss Venable said, opening her eyes. Emily looked up, surprised. "However, it seems apparent that they are no longer in residence. The shades are pulled down, and the windows have been closed all weekend, even though the days are warm, not to say hot. The garbage was not put out. The house is almost certainly empty."

So she had been observing the house, too! Emily searched the old lady's face after her remarkable report but Miss Venable remained inscrutable.

"But how can you really tell if it's vacant?" Emily asked.

"I should imagine a rock through the window would do the trick," Miss Venable said smoothly.

Emily stared at her new ally. "Now," she asked her, "or later, after a few chapters?"

"Later," Miss Venable said, settling herself comfortably into her chair.

Emily began reading. The heroine was named Doreen, an Irish maid who dreamed of being a great lady—an impossible dream in the 1820s in England. But though only a maid for the Wyman family just outside London, Doreen had come from Irish nobility. She was searching for her brother. Miss Venable sighed.

"Excuse me, Miss Crane. This book sounds too much like the one we just finished." She opened a deep drawer in the table next to her and selected a book. "Let's try something more contemporary."

Emily took the book. It was called *The Press of Love*. Emily turned to the first page.

" 'Dana Beacon was twenty-eight and she had given up on love. She wanted only to do her job as a reporter as well as she could, to travel, to be independent. The very manner in which she walked signaled her love of her independence, a swinging jaunt, head high as she moved along the street in Rome. But on the first day that the new city editor, Jim McFarland, took over the European edition of the *New York Globe*, their instant dislike for each other surprised even their coworkers, hardened reporters all.' "

Across the way, in the Carroll Street house, the door to a storeroom on the bottom floor opened and the man who killed Stefan emerged. McKay shut the door behind him and sauntered along the hallway to the worn stairs that led up to the living room. He was smoking a cigarette and smiling his lazy smile.

Emily read about the passionate antipathy between Dana and Jim until lunchtime, when Miss Venable nodded for her to cease.

"Let's throw the rock now," said Miss Venable with energy.

"Right," said Emily, suppressing the urge to laugh out loud.

Using her cane, the old lady climbed out of her chair and started moving off toward the kitchen.

"But once I do that, what's it prove?" asked Emily, following her.

"Certainly not a great deal unless you follow up and get inside."

"I see," said Emily. "I guess I better break one

of the front windows on the street with all the kids watching because there's no way into the backyard."

Miss Venable virtually smirked at Emily. Emily opened the back door. Slowly, the old lady took the backstairs into the serene and sunny garden, picked her way across the grass past her prize tea roses to the wooden fence that divided her property from the Carroll Street house. She pointed her cane at one of the slats.

"Pull on it," she directed Emily.

Emily leaned down. "No, no," Miss Venable hissed at her, "from the top." Emily grabbed the top of the board and yanked. It swung so that it was horizontal like a teeter-totter. "Do the next one just like it, and squeeze through." Emily followed instructions and was, in moments, inside the other yard. She replaced the boards in their original position. She peeked over the top of the fence.

"Miss Venable?"

"Yes?"

"Why is the fence like that?"

"Ahhh," Miss Venable sighed. "I may tell you about Robbie someday. He lived in the Carroll Street house many years ago."

An assignation in Victorian times? Emily thought. What a delicious image, a young Miss Venable stealing into the garden to meet her—lover? Miss Venable was certainly full of surprises today.

The garden had been running wild for some time. The grass was long, the bushes poking out every which way, a stone birdbath almost covered by the hollyhocks and trumpet vines. Emily made her way across the yard to the cement walkway beside the back ground-floor door that led to a kitchen. There, she picked up a rock and threw it through one of the windowpanes in the door. She looked around hastily and listened intently. If anyone in the neighboring gardens had heard, they were not moving to do anything about it. Emily looked back up at Miss Venable's house. Miss Venable was at the big kitchen window. She waved her cane at Emily.

Emily carefully put her arm through the jagged hole in the broken glass pane and unlocked the door.

Upstairs, in an empty room, McKay had heard the crash of the stone through the window and looked down to see Emily, twisting the kitchen doorknob and slipping inside. For several moments, McKay gazed at the spot she'd just left, his flat eyes motionless. Then he stirred himself reluctantly.

Emily felt like an intruder. What would she say if she met someone inside, she wondered. What *could* she say? Anxious and uneasy, she went to the kitchen. It was tidy. She opened the refrigerator. Milk, butter, beer, cheese. The food was fresh.

In the hall, Emily found a door that led, she imagined, to a storeroom, but the door was locked. She tried it several times without success and then gave up. Slowly, she started up the stairs.

The living room was on the floor above ground

level. The curtains were drawn, and the room was stale and hot. The house felt deserted but the food in the refrigerator told her that someone had been here and might be back. Emily raked one set of curtains open and peered out. A stream of light spilled over the furniture in a broad band. Dust motes bobbed in the air. She started to search the room. But she didn't know what she was looking for.

The distant sounds of children playing in the street outside drifted in. She examined a few books in a bookshelf, and the bric-a-brac on the small table. On the mantelpiece, she picked up a small sculpture shaped like a jagged cross. She put it back, then started up the inside staircase to the next floor.

Two spare, neatly made-up bedrooms opened off the landing. She couldn't tell how long ago the rooms had been used, but there was very little dust on the windowsills and the unpainted wood dresser. She sighed. There were no clues that she could see. Then she noticed a closet door. *Ah!* she thought, maybe Stefan left some clothes. She opened the door and within a second was face-to-face with McKay.

The scream of shock and fear gushed out of her like a fountain of sound. Its suddenness wiped the slight smile from his thin lips. Emily turned to flee, then screamed again. Cochran's form filed the doorway.

"That's the man who killed Stefan—" she shrieked, pointing to McKay.

Cochran made a quick move and she threw up

her arm to defend herself, but he was after McKay. He seized the smaller man and pushed him into the wall, but McKay was quick and agile. He slipped out of Cochran's grasp and darted toward the door, where Cochran grabbed him again. McKay's knife flashed upward viciously. Cochran dodged it, and backed away. Emily glanced around the room for a weapon, then rushed to the bed.

At that instant, McKay turned his head toward her, and Cochran closed in, seizing the hand that held the knife and twisting it. McKay grunted, his lips pulled back from his teeth in a terrible grin. They rolled to the floor and the knife went skittering across to the dresser.

By this time, Emily had the bedspread off the bed and was circling behind McKay, ready to throw it over his head at her first opportunity. But the knife was more important, so she dropped the spread and made a dive for the weapon. McKay landed a punch on Cochran's shoulder that made him wince, then, like a dancer, pivoted to reach down and grab the knife. Emily seized it from McKay as Cochran, using his other arm, grabbed a handful of McKay's hair and yanked him back. Emily retreated with the knife as Cochran sent a solid fist into McKay's jaw. But McKay wasn't out yet. He savagely kneed Cochran in the groin. Cochran doubled over in agony and McKay rushed out of the room.

Cochran slipped to the floor, hearing McKay's light footsteps racing down the stairs, followed by the sound of the front door opening and slamming shut.

"Are you all right?" Emily asked, kneeling down.

"I'm fine. I just like lying here." Cochran lifted his head.

Still holding the knife, she went into the bathroom and returned with a wet washcloth, which she placed on his head.

"That's not where I need it," Cochran said, smiling a little.

"He pulled a dirty trick," Emily said.

"I teach dirty tricks," he said bitterly.

Painfully, Cochran got to his feet. He was swaying. Emily reached out to help him balance himself. The touch surprised both of them. She was quite close to him. She saw a bead of perspiration on his wide forehead and then glanced into his eyes. They were as blue as cornflowers, clear and brilliant. She'd never noticed them before.

At her touch, Cochran felt a shiver of desire ripple through him. Neither of them moved, magnetized by the mutual attraction.

Emily drew her hand back. She was the first to regain her footing in their old, adversarial relationship. "What are you doing here?" she asked him.

"You bellyached to the cops about this house," he said, taking his cue from her. But he spoke more roughly than he'd intended. He saw her take another step back. Her cheeks were pink, and her lips moist with exertion. "I thought I'd take a look," he said more gently. All at once he wanted to make love to her and he was shocked at the strength of the urge.

"Of course, it was just a coincidence that I was here," she said, her voice heavily sarcastic. "Of course, you're not following me, are you?"

"Hey, wait a minute! I just saved your life, you want to argue coincidence?" She was still carrying the knife. "Give that to me." He took it from her and examined it. "What about *you* being here?" he asked bluntly. But no matter what he said or she said, it did not erase the tremendous desire he had for her.

"I thought *someone* should look," she replied. "I didn't think the police ever would."

Their words skittered across the ballooning tension between them. She was suddenly aware of his shoulders, of the athletic pitch of his hips and back, of the strong, graceful way he moved. She retreated from him, aware, too, that he was looking at her in a different way.

"We'd better put this place together before we both get arrested." He turned away and began straightening the room.

She picked up the spread from the floor. "Did you search any part of the house?" she asked, watching him.

"I didn't get the chance," he said.

"That basement room is locked," she told him.

He stopped straightening and looked at her. "Oh, ho," he said, shoving the bed back against the wall with his knee. "Let's go."

They both made for the door. At the last moment, he stepped aside for her. His arm came out to guide her protectively but as his fingertips touched her waist, he withdrew. He followed her out.

All the way down the stairs, Emily felt his eyes on her back and waist. She wished she had worn a less revealing summer dress.

Outside the storeroom, Emily tried the door again as Cochran watched. She hammered, banged, rushed into the kitchen, returned with a table knife, depressed it between the jamb and the door. Nothing worked.

"I can't stand amateurs," Cochran said, sighing.

He moved her gently aside. From his pocket, he took out a ring choked with keys, a small implement that looked to Emily like a tiny crochet hook, and a file. He went to work on the door. In a few minutes, it swung open. Cochran smiled at her proudly. Emily rolled her eyes skyward.

The storeroom was filled with odds and ends of furniture, packing cases, cartons of books.

"Why would anyone lock it?" she asked. "There's nothing here anyone would want to steal."

"Maybe, but we don't know that yet for sure." He picked up a lamp shaped like a motor car. "Here's a nice lamp." Emily gave him a withering look. "You have your taste. I have mine," Cochran replied with dignity, replacing the lamp.

"Why lock up a lot of junk?" she repeated, staring at it. She began to prowl around the room, picking up a book, looking inside a box.

Cochran watched her with a different eye now. She moved like a little deer, in bounds, with just a hint of sexuality. Her shapely bare arm reached for a book. He watched her peer at it, her blond hair falling over her cheek. Then she'd return it to a box and leap away at some other target of interest. She had a narrow waist; on her feet were open sandals. Her feet were beautiful; long slender toes, elegant ankles. His eyes traveled up her back to the nape of her neck. He imagined himself kissing her, holding her against his body.

"You hungry?" he asked, and when she didn't answer, "I'm getting my appetite back."

She spotted the red cover of Stefan's book in one carton. Instinctively, she turned to shield the discovery from Cochran. "Did you hear something?" she asked.

"Nope," he said, still enjoying watching her.

"I thought I heard a voice," she lied.

As he turned his back and moved to the door, Emily removed Stefan's book and stuffed it into her purse. Cochran turned back, shaking his head.

"I don't hear a thing," he said.

"It must have been from the garden," she said.

They faced each other in the small, closed space. Emily felt unexpectedly drawn to him at that moment—a thing she'd never imagined could happen. She wanted to touch him again, but she knew if she did, she would not be able to stop.

"I'm sorry about the other night in your apart-

ment," Cochran said. "What I said to you."
Emily didn't answer. "Wasn't any reason to get
personal." His apology was simple and direct
and handsome. There was more to this man
than she'd thought.

"I was personal, too," she admitted.

"Yeah, but you're not sorry," he said, smiling.
Emily laughed. "I'd just like to have dinner with
you. That's the long and the short of it. No other
reason," he lied.

"I'm not hungry," Emily said.

"You can watch me! It's a sight. People have
paid money," he teased her. He felt happy, and
he realized that he hadn't felt that way since he
arrived in New York three years ago.

"I can see that at the zoo," she said. "Anyway,
I have to go back and tell Miss Venable I'm
safe."

"We can do that," he said, liking her sense of
responsibility, "and then we'll go eat." He did
not want to leave her now.

Chapter 9

Emily was watching Mike Cochran eat. They sat at a secluded table in the back of an elegant Chinese restaurant on 125th Street and Broadway. Steaming dishes were piled before them. She sipped her tea as he handled chopsticks like a virtuoso.

"That's amazing," she said with a reluctant respect as he dipped his chopsticks into a multi-colored pile of food and fished out a tiny strand of ginger. Mike Cochran might be many things, but he was not ordinary.

A elderly waiter in a white jacket arrived with two more dishes—duck and something with green pea pods.

"And the shrimp dish?" Cochran asked the waiter. "The one with the little red things in it?" The waiter nodded, his eyes twinkling, and left. Cochran plucked some pea pods out of the dish and placed them in his rice bowl. The waiter returned with the shrimp. Cochran raised his eyebrows and waved his hand over the shrimp to waft its sweet and sour scent toward him.

Suddenly Mike Cochran, the simple midwesterner, started speaking to the waiter in fluent Chinese. Emily felt her jaw drop. The waiter's formal air of indifference vanished. He laughed melodiously, responding in a stream of Chinese. He obviously knew and liked Cochran, who was commenting on something the waiter had said. The waiter answered and went off chuckling.

Her distrust of him showed all over her wary face. Cochran knew he was going to have to tell her everything; he was going to have to open up in a way he rarely offered anyone. He smiled mischievously at Emily, anticipating her first question.

"The army. Taught me Chinese for two years. I've got a natural aptitude for languages." He scooped up shrimp, pea pods, and rice and thrust them into his mouth. Swallowing, he went on, "Afterward, of course, they sent me to Germany. That's called the army way. There's the right way, the wrong way, and the army way. They teach you Chinese and send you to Germany."

"How did we win the war?" she asked, sarcastically.

"We had civilians like me!" He ate some more duck. "Now, you want to know how come the FBI." He leaned back in his chair and looked at the ceiling briefly. "The FBI. Ever since I saw James Cagney in *G-Men*. What a movie! I saw it eighteen times!"

"Typical," she said. She folded her arms across her chest. "And do you like what you do, Mr. Cochran?"

"Please call me Mike," he said. "I wouldn't do my work if I didn't like it." He passed her one of the dishes. "Here, try these."

"What are they?" she asked dubiously.

"If you knew, you wouldn't eat them," he said.

She took a fork, speared one of the little circular pieces, and gingerly tasted it. It wasn't bad. "What is it?" she repeated.

"Shark," he said, returning to his food again.

"*Shark!*"

"That's right. Full of protein. Eat up."

She put her fork down. "I don't eat shark," she said. She had even less appetite than before.

"I'd like you to know more about me," he said. Her expression softened. "I didn't grow up respectable," he confided. "Like you."

"We weren't that respectable," she said, but didn't reveal anything else.

"My old man was a drunk. I watched him die on the vine. You heard about the Depression." He paused.

Nodding, she said, "Even in Connecticut." She was trying to stop liking him. She wanted to go back to the old animosity, the old natural disdain for the FBI, and for him.

"The point is," he went on, "I've got nothing to love this country for. It never gave me a thing. It just took. Dried up my mother and took her when I was nine. It hammered my old man down and then threw him away." He stabbed his chopsticks into his rice bowl. "The war saved me, you know that? Without it, I would have been a small-town bum," he said, smiling crookedly at the memory. He looked at her with his clear blue eyes. "I loved World War Two. I didn't want it to stop. The army discovered my aptitudes. Nobody had ever done that before," he said. "Nobody'd cared. When I got out of the army, I went to law school, got my degree." Suddenly he stopped talking, glanced down at his chopsticks, and wiggled them a bit. He felt self-conscious about revealing himself that much.

Emily leaned forward and poured herself another cup of tea. "What am I doing here with you?"

"Nothing you don't want to do," he said. He started eating again.

I don't even like this guy, she thought, *what's-his-name, Mike.* She watched him manipulate the chopsticks. His fingers were long and dexterous, his wrists limber. *This guy is a fascist,* she thought. *He's against everything I stand for. He wouldn't understand the Constitution of this country if I read it to him word for word. He agrees with searching people's homes under flimsy pretexts.*

Yet she couldn't help smiling. She wanted to tell him about Jeff, about how he died, about how guilty she felt, about how chilly her mother had been, and about her father. But she delayed the impulse.

He ate on. *He was right,* she thought. *People would pay to watch him eat.* "I feel like I'm watching a state-fair contest," she said. He laughed.

* * *

Cochran pulled his car to a stop in front of her apartment building and shut off the engine.

"I'll stay here until you get inside," he said. "Just come to the window and wave."

"Thank you. Thank you for letting me watch you eat dinner. Such a remarkable evening. Does it go on the expense account?" She touched his arm and felt him stiffen. "I apologize, I didn't mean that. I don't know what to make of you," she said honestly.

"What you see is what you get," he replied.

"You've got a great act, Cochran," she said. She was afraid it was an act, that he was trying to trick her into trusting him. But why? He stirred next to her. Her unwanted attraction to him rose in her again.

Cochran felt her nearness like a heat, spreading from her to him in waves. He knew she felt it too.

"Good night," Emily said. She didn't want to leave and she didn't want to stay.

"Good night," he said. "*Oh.* Almost forgot. You want to give me that book you lifted back there at the house?"

She glared at him. He'd broken the soft moment that had held them both. He shrugged, smiling his half smile again. "Dinner's over," he explained.

"I see," she said, feeling foolish. She took a book from her purse and slapped it into his hand.

"That's what you took?" he asked.

"Yes," she lied.

"Emily Dickinson," he said in disbelief.

"There it is," she said. "Fascinating, isn't it?"
He handed it back to her. "You have many sides, Miss Crane," he said. He knew it wasn't the same book.

She put the book back in her purse, wondering if she had put one over on him. She doubted it.

He watched Emily open the front door and disappear inside. He didn't think she was in grave danger, but she was in some danger, and he was sure she was being watched. He waited, looking at her window until her light went on. He waited. *Is she going to do it?* he wondered, feeling the intense eagerness again in his almost illicit connection to her. Finally, he saw her come to the window, but she didn't wave or even look out. She stood against it, backlit by the room. Then she pulled the shade down, shutting him out. He ached to be near her again.

Emily sat down on her living-room couch and took out Stefan's book. She shook it to see if anything was inside and flipped quickly through the pages. Nothing fell out, no piece of paper had been hidden there. She opened it to the flyleaf. In a curly, slanted penmanship, someone had written the name and a date: "Laura Moulton, 1851."

The writing meant nothing to her. She leafed carefully through the book, looking for notes in the margins, underlined words, anything. Not a single mark had been added to the book. She turned back to the title page. *Poems and Tales of Edgar Allan Poe*. Below that came the name of the publishing house and date of publication:

1912. *Hum,* she thought. But the date under Laura Moulton's name is 1851. Was "Laura Moulton" and the date a message?

Deep, dark clouds pressed down upon the humid city as Emily stood with a crowd at a bus stop early the next morning. Her mother had phoned to say she was coming into the city for an eastern seaboard teachers conference. Her mother had reminded Emily to buy an umbrella because a storm was coming.

Emily didn't like umbrellas and always managed to lose them. Umbrellas were not uppermost in her mind anyway this morning; Cochran was, and the Laura Moulton conundrum. She had managed to make her feelings last night for Mike Cochran retreat; it was easier when she called him "the fascist FBI midwesterner." But his blue eyes and the naked interest in them—the intelligence of the man—kept intruding. She tried to take her mind off both Laura Moulton and Mike Cochran by guessing where the people waiting for the bus with her worked.

"We'd like to talk to you, Miss Crane."

She jumped and turned. Cochran and Hackett were right in back of her.

"Very sneaky," she said bitingly, looking at Cochran, who wouldn't meet her eyes. They were so obviously "the law" that the other people waiting there instinctively shrank away from Emily. "I've been waiting for you to show up," she said. "It saves me a phone call."

She took Stefan's book from her purse. Far up the block she could see the bus approaching.

"Here's the book." Cochran's hand touched hers as she handed him the book. She looked up into his clear blue eyes and smiled. He *had* known about the book, as she'd suspected. "It was owned by someone named Laura Moulton," Emily said. "Open it up." He did so. "See? She wrote her name and then the date—1851." They looked at the title page. "But the book was printed in 1912. So she couldn't possibly have written this in 1851. What does it mean? I can't figure it out, but I know"—she dropped her voice—"that it has to do with Stefan's murder. What was he doing that he thought was so bad and so dangerous that he wanted to escape?" They didn't respond. "Instead of following me around, why don't you find out? Do something useful for a change," she said, looking Mike Cochran in the eyes.

The bus arrived, and Emily got on with the others. Cochran looked after the bus as it pulled away in a cloud of dense exhaust. He felt miserable. She was back to hating him again. He looked at the small red book in his hand.

"Back off, Mike," Hackett said, "While you still got time."

"What're your talking about?" Cochran said, not looking at him.

"I mean it. She's poison." He clapped Cochran on the shoulder. "C'mon, we got a date with the lab." He snapped his finger against the book in Cochran's hand.

"'Dana couldn't get Jim out of her mind,'" Emily was reading. Miss Venable, in a dark red dress, sat in her chair, her eyes closed. "'Dana had been staring at her typewriter and the half-finished story about the public library cleaning lady who'd lost her job. She tossed her curly chestnut hair and attacked the typewriter. But she could still feel Jim's arms around her on the ferry, the pleasing bulk of him, the protection of him. Most of all, she was shocked that a man she considered an enemy could, almost overnight, become a lover.'"

Miss Venable raised her hand. "The story bores me," she said, "compared to your adventures in that house yesterday. Tell me more about Mr. Cochran. I do not trust the reasons he was so conveniently in the house. Do you?"

"No," Emily said, putting the book aside. "I don't either. I'm—I'm afraid to trust him."

"Very wise," said Miss Venable. She leaned forward in her chair, putting both hands on her cane and using it as a support. "Let's go through it again," she said, her eyes sparkling. "Maybe there's something we missed."

Cochran and Hackett were sitting in a booth at a Blarney Stone bar. A pair of beers and juicy, overstuffed sandwiches were on the table in front of them. It was about five o'clock in the afternoon, and the bar was crowded with noisy regulars who were reliving the last game between the Brooklyn Dodgers and the New York Giants. Both teams had cheering sections in the bar. Hackett was reading the sports pages of a newspaper. Cochran was lifting half his sandwich to his mouth and studying the flyleaf of Stefan's book.

"The ink is modern," Cochran mumbled. "Waterman's, you can buy it anywhere. The lab figures it was written within the year." He bit into his sandwich.

Buried in the paper, Hackett said, "Look at this. The Duke went four for four."

Cochran wasn't listening. He stared at the flyleaf of the book. "Now, what's so special about 1851? Poe died in 1849, I looked it up. What do you think?" Cochran asked Hackett.

"I think he'll win the batting title going away," Hackett said, totally wrapped up in his paper.

"Who?" Cochran demanded.

"Duke Snider," Hackett said.

Shaking his head, Cochran said, "He'll never catch Musial." Rapping the back of his knuckles on the book, Cochran said, "The book, Hackett, the book. Suppose it isn't a year? I mean, suppose it's a day, a month and a year. One. Eight. Fifty-one. January eighth, 1951. Yeah, how about that?"

"That's been and gone," Hackett said, without interest.

"But, look at the handwriting. It's not American," Cochran said.

"So?" Hackett said, not following.

"Americans put the month first, Europeans put the day. So it could also mean the first day of the eighth month. August first, 1951," Cochran said.

"That's tomorrow. We play the Cubs," Hackett added.

"She could be on to something," Cochran said, brightening.

"You're a dumb hick, you know that?" said Hackett, folding up his paper and putting his elbow on the table. "You still believe the Giants are going to win the pennant." He smiled grimly. "Why else did they tell us to lean on her?"

"Do you know why?" Cochran asked.

Hackett shook his head. "I know only two things. The Dodgers are going to win and what I learned in the navy. Keep your mouth shut, your bowels open, and never volunteer."

"A guy's been murdered," Cochran protested.

"There is a police department for such matters," Hackett reminded him.

"She could have been next if I hadn't been there."

"So you're a hero. You and Stan Musial. Now, lay off or they'll have your head on a plate," Hackett warned.

"She's in trouble, Sid," Cochran said.

"That doesn't mean you have to commit suicide," Hackett replied. "She's a red, she's all balled up in God knows what-all. Leave it alone."

"I like her," Cochran admitted.

Hackett stared at him, considering his partner more carefully. "You want to make a little wager?" Hackett finally asked him.

"We're already betting on the pennant," Cochran said.

"On the batting title. You got Musial, I take Snider," Hackett challenged.

"And you call me dumb?" Cochran laughed.

"Deal?" Hackett said.

"Deal," Cochran replied.

Hackett took a long pull from his beer, then reached over and took the book from Cochran. He was going to give Cochran a lesson.

"You've got a woman's name and a date. Tomorrow. Something special tomorrow. The lady's birthday? A rendezvous someplace? A love nest? But for a rendezvous, you don't put down the year. You figure you know what year it is. So maybe it's not a woman," Hackett said.

"But what else could it be?" Cochran asked.

Hackett looked at him, disappointed.

Chapter 10

The huge freighter looked old and battered as two diminutive tugs slowly guided it into the slip at Pier 29. About thirty passengers crowded its rails, looking down on the scanty group of friends or relatives who waited below. The name of the side of the ship was the *Laura Moulton*.

"Thanks for calling," Emily said to Cochran. She couldn't keep the begrudging note out of her voice. "How did you figure out it was a ship?" Some of the people in the crowd surrounding them held up signs with names scrawled on them. Emily had already looked for the names connected to her "situation," as she had come to call it.

"I've got a smart partner," he said.

"Why are you doing this?" Emily asked.

"Would you like it better if I didn't?" he asked, and then abruptly changed the subject, "I checked the manifest. She's carrying furniture and refugees."

"Refugees from where?" she asked

"Germany, mostly. Some from behind the Iron Curtain. All of them have been checked and double-checked. They are exactly who their papers say they are. The cargo was shaken down by experts before it was loaded. But that's all routine." He scanned the people around them. He leaned close to her. An aroma like nutmeg and a summery perfume clung to her hair. "Do any of these people look familiar?" he asked.

Emily shook her head. The passengers were assembling in a line, coming forward in turn to be processed by Immigration. People looked bored as well as excited, a curious, almost untenable mixture of emotions, she thought. The officials from Immigration moved slowly, attending to their innumerable fine-print regulations.

Emily saw one Immigration officer split off three men from the crowd of passengers. He sent them to one side where they stood by themselves. They were in their thirties, she judged, and seemed no different from the others, yet the official was treating them with more than the usual courtesy. Emily puzzled about it until she saw Matilde approaching the men.

"Cochran," Emily whispered urgently. "Cochran, the woman!" Excited, Emily pulled at Cochran's jacket. "I know that woman. Matilde's her name. I saw her with Stefan on Carroll Street in front of the house!"

Now an official-looking man came up to Matilde and the three men. He was about fifty, had gray hair, a black mustache, and large pale eyes framed by rimless glasses. He shook hands formally with Matilde, and then introduced himself, shaking hands with each of the men. He pointed out an exit door.

"Come on!" Emily said. But Cochran hung back. "We have to follow them!"

He didn't move. His face was a mask. "Uh-uh," Cochran said.

"Why not?" she asked.

Gesturing, he said, "See that guy?" He waved casually at a tall man with prematurely white hair.

"Yes," Emily said, "so what?"

"That's Simpson and he's government. Whatever this is, it's official," Cochran informed her. Bob Simpson was well known in government circles. He'd worked with Donovan in the OSS, the precursor of the CIA. In some ways, he was a maverick, and had often represented the CIA on unofficial company business. "He watches after their interests," Cochran said. Simpson's presence put real power behind whatever was going on here.

"You're official, aren't you! Aren't you government?" she asked him hotly.

"Not like Simpson," he replied.

"Who's that other official-looking guy, the one with the black mustache with Matilde?"

"Beats me, Lieutenant," he said. "But he's obviously been sent here to meet them and get them all through with no fuss. Those three guys are important, no kidding."

"Official—does that mean you'll stand for anything? Does that mean you'll quit?!" she demanded. "Official just makes it worse!"

"Will you pipe down?" he hissed, looking around.

The official man and Matilde had moved outside the glass doors, escorting the three strangers to an unmarked dark sedan.

"Cochran! Tom, Dick, and Harry are getting away!"

"Who?" he asked crossly.

"The three strangers who got off the boat. Don't quit on me," she pleaded. "Please."

The church was onion-domed, its spires topped by four unusual crosses. It sat on a corner lot in a leafy, sun-dappled neighborhood in Connecticut. A bride and groom were coming down the church steps with a dignified and fully bearded priest who looked as if he'd stepped out of another age. Certainly out of another culture. Exuberant wedding guests surrounded the three central characters in this small but moving drama. The procession stopped momentarily for a photo, then moved into the enclosed garden next to the church for the reception. Laughing and shouting guests were already clustered around a huge buffet table, laden with exotic foods. Others tapped their feet at the edge of a temporary dance floor, poised with the waiting orchestra for the celebration to begin in earnest.

The black sedan carrying the three refugees, the official man with the black mustache, and Matilde, glided past the wedding party like a shark in shallow water. Slowly, it slid out of sight around the corner.

"Won't they see us?" Emily asked Cochran as they followed the sedan in Cochran's nondescript FBI-issue car.

"Nah," said Mike. "We're late guests."

Emily looked toward the garden as they went by. Accompanied by the richly dressed priest, the bride and groom were moving to the center of the crowd where a group of beaming relatives were waiting for them. "It's so touching," Emily whispered. "I love weddings." She looked up at the spires. "Isn't this a Russian Orthodox church?" she asked Mike as they rounded the corner.

"I think so." He turned into an all-American street that shone with innocent virtues. It was shaded by giant maple trees. The black sedan was parked next to a back gate of the garden.

Emily shuddered. The sedan seemed sinister. "Well," she said in a false bright voice, "how do you like it?"

"Like what?"

"Mapleton, Connecticut! I was born a few miles from here, but you see one town in this part of the state, you've seen them all. Maybe we should stop on the way back and visit Mom."

Cochran halted his car in the shadow of the large trees. In the garden, under the priest's supervision, a short ceremony was taking place. It involved the giving of bread and salt. "I think they're Ukrainian," Mike said carefully, glimpsing the stiff bridal headdress and looking at the bright printed gowns of the women. "We've fallen right into a hotbed of Reds—how do you like that?"

"Do you guys really think every Russian is bent on overthrowing the U.S. government?" she demanded, angry at him and at herself for forgetting the great differences that separated them. "That bride doesn't look like an anarchist to me!"

"Where's your sense of humor?" he snapped. At that moment, Tom, Dick, and Harry got out of the sedan, followed by the other man and Matilde. As they entered the garden, two people from the wedding party rushed over to greet them happily. A great shout of joy came from the guests: the toast had been drunk. Glasses were thrown to the floor. The band struck up a rousing polka number, and in seconds, the floor was filled with whirling dancers.

"Are you game?" Emily asked.

"This is very dangerous," he said, glancing at her, trying to figure out how he could dissuade her. "What are you doing?"

Emily was braiding her long hair. She grinned at him as she took a few bobby pins out of her handbag and pinned the braids up on top of her head. "I'm camouflaging myself for the Ukrainian party. Didn't you notice the women?" She whipped out a lipstick and compact, and smeared her lips generously with the bright color. She rouged her cheeks heavily. Cochran sighed deeply. Then he saw Simpson enter the garden.

"You're running a special risk here, Emily," he said seriously. He nodded at Simpson. "That guy is unofficially from the CIA, remember? It means that whatever's going on here, it has official sanction. He knows me. And that woman Matilde knows you. If she recognizes you, the first assumption anyone's going to make is that you have an ulterior motive." He didn't mention that if Simpson recognized him, he could be suspended for interfering.

"I don't get you," said Emily, spreading the rouge on her cheeks.

"Because of your record with the investigating committee," he said through his teeth. "They won't believe you're out here for the reason I think you're out here."

"And what's that?" she said, snapping her compact closed.

"The boy. He touched you somewhere very deep, and you feel responsible for his death." He turned to face her. "But you're not! Emily, let's drive away. Nothing's—"

She opened her door of the car and stepped out. Full of misgivings, he followed her into the garden.

Cochran looked around the crowd uneasily and spotted Simpson on the other side of the garden. His six-foot frame and white hair made him an easy man to keep in view. Cochran moved to a spot beside a large clipped Eugenia hedge behind Simpson. The last thing he wanted was to be recognized. He had a bad feeling about being here.

He watched Emily sail briskly into the crowd. She looked just like a late-arriving guest—eager and apologetic at the same time.

Cochran's eye settled on one of the men from the boat. He was heaping his plate with food from the buffet table. The man's eyes bulged out as he ladled salads, snatched up breads, and speared meats. Emily, with her upswept hair and her painted, vivid smile, took a place in the line behind him. Cochran chuckled. She looked like she belonged there. Emily was intrepid, there was no other word for her. Had she fainted or cowered during that fight with McKay? Nope. She had been down on the floor grabbing for the knife! She had courage and character—the combination increased his desire for her tenfold.

Emily was right behind the gluttonous man from the boat. She saw him stop reaching for food, heft his plate, and move away from the buffet table. But as Emily turned to follow him, a hand fell heavily on her shoulder.

"Freda, am I right?" she heard a man say.

She turned. A huge, very cheerful, and very drunk young man was looking down at her, grinning like a lunatic. He had masses of black hair and a big jaw.

"Nope," she replied, and tried to move away, but he was not so easily put off.

"Celia? Celia Ostrovsky," he tried again.

Keeping her eyes on the man from the boat—Emily had dubbed him "Tom"—she said, "Try again."

"I never forget a face," the man growled morosely, "but I'm not so hot on names." He frowned, thinking hard. It was an effort. "Stephanie?"

Emily saw Matilde walking in her direction. She quickly turned her back on the room and took the huge man's arm. "Connie," she said, smiling broadly at him.

"Sure, that's who! Connie! You're a friend of Stephanie's. I remember you. Remember me? I'm Stash," he said.

Matilde was moving closer, and then passing them. She didn't even notice Emily.

"Oh, yeah," Emily said, relieved. "Stash."

"Where you been, Connie?" he whined, a strange sound from such a large man. "I ain't seen you around lately."

Matilde was walking away from them. "I moved," Emily said.

"Yeah, well, I don't blame you. This town is a dump. You want to dance, Connie?" Stash asked her.

Matilde was crossing to Simpson, the tall, white-haired government official. She started talking to him, chopping the air with her hand.

"No, thanks. Maybe later," Emily said to Stash.

"I gotta dance now," Stash said truculently. "Later I ain't even gonna be able to stand up."

"Tom" was sitting down next to "Dick" from the boat.

"Well, look me up if you can make it, Stash," Emily said sympathetically. "I got to meet my friends." She flashed him a smile, and balancing her plate, she pushed her way through the crowd toward Tom and Dick. Her heart was pounding. She hoped Mike hadn't lost track of her in the manic celebrations—the crowd was getting more boisterous every minute. She strode up directly in front of Tom and Dick, and displayed her most powerful smile.

"It's a wonderful party, isn't it?" she said.

Tom looked at her, panic skating across his face. He turned to the man beside him and muttered something in another language. Dick smiled politely at Emily. He had sandy hair and hazel eyes. Dick was a good deal tougher than Tom.

"Please?" Dick asked.

"I said, it's a wonderful party, isn't it?" she repeated.

"Oh yes," Dick said with a heavy accent. "Very wonderful."

"How was your trip? Was it smooth?" she said.

Nodding, Dick said, "Oh, yes. Very smooth."

"I'm sorry, I forgot my manners. I'm Connie Ostrovsky," Emily said, pretending to be contrite.

Drawing himself up, Dick said, "Sackadorf."

"Sackadorf?" she stuttered.

"Yes," Sackadorf said.

Emily turned to Tom, doing her best to conceal her excitement.

"And you must be Mr. Bistrong," she guessed.

"Hurwitz," Tom replied. She suspected that his name was the only "English" word he knew.

Emily plunged forward. "And how is Dr. Teperson? Have you spoken to him since your arrival?"

"I am Teperson," a voice came from behind her.

Emily felt her back stiffen. She turned. Not two feet away from her was the short, balding man she'd seen—and who had seen her—through the window in the house on Carroll Street.

Chapter 11

Dr. Teperson stared at Emily as if he were thinking of dissecting her. "Do I know you?" he asked.

Not really, she thought, *but you sure know how to speak English!*

With perfect manners, Dick said, "Dr. Teperson. Miss Ostrovsky."

"Oh . . . ah, yes, of course," cried Emily. "Mrs.—you know her name . . ." Emily gestured vaguely, "She introduced us. I'm flattered you remembered, there were so many people . . ." On the pretense of looking around for the woman who'd "introduced" them, she scanned the crowd for Cochran. She was frightened.

"I was thinking we had met—before today," Teperson said, a note of suspicion creeping into his voice.

"No. I don't think so," Emily said. "I certainly would have remembered."

Emily spotted Cochran across a sea of dancing bodies. He was looking for her. "Oh! There's Olaf!" she smiled at Dr. Teperson. "Excuse me."

She darted away from them and skirted across the dance floor in a beeline for Cochran. "Oh God, I'm so glad I found you," she breathed, taking his arm and leading him onto the dance floor. "Don't turn around," she said. "The short paunchy one with the men from the boat, he's the one I saw through the window."

"What window?" asked Cochran.

"The window in the garden."

"What garden?"

She pulled back and looked at him. "The garden in Brooklyn," she said, annoyed. *"Oh, I'm* sorry, I told all that to Lieutenant Sloan. I get you official guys all mixed up, don't I?"

Cochran looked over her shoulder, suddenly aware that he was dancing with her, holding her around the waist, gripping her hand, feeling her breasts nudge against his chest. Emily was babbling on about the house on Carroll Street and Teperson. The two men from the boat were talking to each other, but Teperson was watching Emily.

"He recognized me," Emily said, "but I don't think he knows from where." She let herself fall into the rhythm of the dance, feeling Mike's leg against hers and his arm around her waist. "Sackadorf's over there, and Hurwitz—" Suddenly she stopped.

He stumbled. "What's—"

"Cochran, I've figured it out," she said in an excited whisper.

"Keep dancing," he said.

"These men—Stefan had their names in his pocket and I saw him getting names from the

158

cemetery. Dead people, Cochran. They've been smuggled in as people who are dead!''

"Keep dancing," Cochran said, tightly.

"Is that all you can say? Who are they, Cochran?"

"Ukrainian," Cochran said, smiling at her.

"Maybe, but not Teperson. He speaks German. Of course, Tom, Dick, and Harry are Ukrainian. We know that. But why do they have to be smuggled in? What are they?"

"People who can't get in normally," Cochran said, still watching the men.

"Why can't they get in normally? Which side were they on over there?"

Cochran saw Matilde and the official with the black mustache approach the men for a huddled conversation. Teperson was animated; they all glanced briefly at Emily and Cochran.

Cochran stopped dancing. "Why are you stopping?" asked Emily.

"I think we'd better get out of here," he said. He took her arm and, smiling, they started working their way through the dancers. Emily couldn't help looking back over her shoulder. Matilde was leading the men across the lawn and into the church.

"Wait! We have to find out—" she said.

"Not now," Cochran said, tightening his hold on her arm. "We're outnumbered."

Stash came up to them. "Connie?" he said drunkenly, holding out his arms. Emily accepted with alacrity, shaking free of Cochran. He watched her do one spin with Stash, then make some excuse and start across the lush lawn toward the church. "Damn!" Cochran said, following her.

"Cochran!"

Mike turned. "Hello, Simpson!" Cochran said jovially, sticking out his hand. Simpson didn't take it.

"You part of the wedding?" Simpson asked. "Relatives or something?" His black eyes had always reminded Cochran of onyx studs.

"Kind of," Cochran said guardedly, looking off toward the church.

With some suspicion, Simpson asked, "You here officially? This is hands-off for you people, you know that." He followed Mike's gaze but Emily had slipped inside the church. Simpson went on: "I can make things very tough if you're here on some kind of rogue fishing expedition." He had a thin cold voice that sounded like air leaking out of a tire.

Cochran smiled warmly. "Nah, Bob," he said. "Bride's a cousin to my stepsister. Told her I'd look in. Want a drink?"

Inside, the church was richly ornamented, the icons and plaster Christs painted in vivid colors and trimmed with gleaming gold. The altar and pews were empty, but a door on the far side was open, and from it came the faint sound of voices.

As Emily was about to start across to it, one of the front doors of the church opened. She popped into a recess and pressed herself against the wall. Peeking out, she saw Matilde come in, cross to the other open door, and disappear.

Emily came out of her hiding place and tiptoed across the floor. The open door led to a lower level. She started down the steps but stopped when she heard voices from below. Matilde and one of the officials from Immigration were speaking; someone else was translating what they said into Russian or Ukranian, Emily couldn't tell which.

"Unfortunately," Matilde was saying, "it has become impossible to use the house any longer. You'll have to spend tonight here and leave for Chicago tomorrow. That will be on the Chicago express, which leaves at six o'clock."

Murmurs and questions greeted her words.

"There's nothing to worry about," a man said. "In Chicago, you will receive your new identities, so it will be impossible to trace you. Then you'll be driven to the installation where—" His voice dropped.

Emily strained to hear from her perch on the stairs. Someone's heels were clicking on the stone flooring of the church. She started back up the stairs, but the footsteps were too close. She shrank back, looking for someplace to hide. The basement door opened back onto the steps; she ducked behind it. There was not much room and she was forced to teeter on the edge of the steps.

Through the crack between the door and the hinge, she saw Simpson start down the steps. She knew then that she had gone too far. Her hands were perspiring and her heart was pounding loudly. When Simpson was out of sight below, Emily shakily crept out from behind the

door. But her foot slipped from her unstable
perch and she started to fall. She clutched at the
door, scraped her knuckles against it, but only
succeeded only in pushing it away from her. It
banged shut with a great clang. She winced. For
an instant, the voices below ceased. Emily felt a
tremendous spurt of fear pump through her.
Someone was starting up the steps toward her in
a dead rush.

She wrenched the door open, raced through
the church and out into the garden, frantically
looking for Cochran. But the only person she
recognized was Stash, helping himself to a couple of chicken legs. Behind her, Simpson was
rushing out of the church. She hurried up to
Stash, forcing a big smile.

"Hey, Stash! You're still on your feet! Let's
dance!" she cried enthusiastically.

The band was playing a vigorous polka. Stash
held up his drumstick. She grabbed him, tossed
his chicken leg away, and dragged him onto the
dance floor. Glancing back at the church, she
saw that Simpson had started back in. She
sighed with relief and smiled up at Stash as he
stepped on her foot.

"You're a wonderful dancer," she said, looking
into his little eyes.

Stash was clumsy but he seemed willing.
Emily smiled up at him, feeling demented and
phony as she tried to look enthralled.

Suddenly he stopped dancing. "Why'd you
stop?" she asked, still smiling up at him.

Stash's big square face had hardened. She

looked around. The official with the black mustache, Simpson, and Matilde stared back at her. "Oh," said Emily. Stash had danced her over to them. Emily was boxed in; there was no escape. "Stash," she said, disappointed. He shrugged his mountainous shoulders.

From a corner of the garden, Cochran watched them escort Emily to a car. He was angry and frustrated, but there was nothing he could do now. He could only follow them and hope for the best.

He went back to his car, got in, and turned on the engine. The black sedan in which they'd unceremoniously shoved Emily was pulling out. Cochran put his car in gear.

A hand shot through his open window and neatly plucked the key out of the ignition. He looked up: Simpson.

"You're out of your jurisdiction," Simpson said, his voice like a cold wind next to Cochran's ear.

It was night. The car carrying Emily streaked along the highway. Emily huddled in the backseat trying hard not to look frightened. A man whose neck and head had no visible division between them was driving the car as though they only had fifteen minutes to make Nebraska. A small cap sat on top of his bullet-shaped head like a cherry. She wished she had a cigarette more than anything else in the world and thought of asking Bullet Head for one. But she didn't want to give him the satisfaction of refusing. He probably didn't understand English anyway. But the need for a cigarete kept clawing at her. She tried to take her mind off it and remembered that her mother was arriving tomorrow. The thought made her titter nervously. How could she have a life that included lunch at Schrafft's and kidnapping the night before?

She was mentally trying out various pronounciations of *cigarette* when Bullet Head pulled up at the "21" club. The doorman immediately pounced on the car and opened the door. Amazed, Emily got out. "I'm not dressed for this," she said to Bullet Head. He didn't even look around. "Miss Crane," said a suave-looking man in a costly suit. "My name's Binney," he said. He took her arm and led her into the restaurant.

The club was filled with the great and the near great. She immediately recognized Robert Taylor and Claudette Colbert and Gary Cooper, sitting at separate tables. The mayor of New York was at the biggest booth. Binney hurried her along to a favored corner banquette where a man sat alone. She saw the back of his head, his thick sandy hair . . .."

It was Salwen. He was all by himself. He smiled up at her, and indicated a seat. Stunned, she sat. A glittering couple came past the banquette and nodded at Salwen, smiling warmly. Salwen returned their greeting, and at the same time, caught the eye of a man farther down the row, to whom he waved faintly. The man acknowledged it generously, then whispered to his bejeweled companion.

Emily swallowed and straightened her wrinkled cotton skirt nervously. Salwen was holding court. She reminded herself that kings at court had the power of life and death.

Chapter 12

"I recommend the hamburger," Salwen said. "No kidding. It's not like you think hamburger. It happens to be famous." Salwen was wearing an impressively cut tuxedo over his broad shoulders. Ruby cuff links sparkled quietly at his wrists.

"No, thanks," Emily replied, gripping her purse. The restaurant was air conditioned, and she felt chilled after the sultry night air.

"How do you like it? Medium, medium rare?" he asked as if she'd said nothing at all.

"Nothing, please," Emily said.

"'From nothing comes nothing.' Shakespeare —that's *King Lear*. Oh," he said airily, "I have a head full of useless quotations." He turned his attention languidly to a hovering waiter. "Medium rare." He swung back to Emily. "Do you prefer cottage fries?" He didn't wait for an answer. To the waiter, he said, "The lady will have cottage fries."

The waiter backed up a few steps as if leaving royalty. Salwen poured Emily a glass of wine.

"Emily," he said with a sigh. "Nobody wants to hurt you. I tried to make that plain before." He tented his manicured fingers, putting his elbows on the table. "There's been too much strong-arm stuff already. So unnecessary. People panic so easily." He sighed again, then picked up his wineglass. He tasted the liquid gingerly, raised his eyebrows, and smiled. "I'm offering you a bargain. One hundred percent clearance. The FBI off your case, you don't have to give us any names, or the Liberty Watch membership list. . . ." He looked down at the beautiful white tablecloth. "Anyway, just between you and me, we got that list a long time ago," Salwen admitted. "There isn't anything the committee—or someone—doesn't have." He looked at her, admiring her beautiful face.

"Do you mean," she began, finding her voice and feeling her anger spill over her fear, "that poor Metzger killed himself and you put me through that hell for something you already had?"

"Oh, was it hell?" he asked in an astonished, innocent voice. He didn't bother commenting on Metzger. "Well, it's not a matter of giving the information requested. It's a matter of giving cooperation to the committee. Didn't you know that?" He smiled and looked at her as if she puzzled him. As he suspected, she didn't say anything. "All I want in return is a simple truth from you." He let that sink in. Then he asked, his eyes piercing the air, "Who else knows?"

Emily looked over the restaurant, watching Gary Cooper and his wife at a nearby booth.

They were smoking and drinking highballs. She didn't want to give Salwen an easy victory or let on how frightened she was of him. She looked boldly back at him and said nothing.

Salwen began again gently, "Alan, Marilyn? That woman you read to? Think—before you speak."

Emily swallowed and put her hands on the table, willing them to keep from trembling. "I'll make a deal with you," she said. Salwen waited. His eyes narrowed minutely. "I'll tell you who knows. And you'll . . . . . ." she went on, taking a deep breath, "you'll tell me who ordered that boy to be killed."

"Curiosity killed the cat, Emily," Salwen said, lightly shaking his finger at her. "That boy was killed years ago. No one survives such a childhood. The camps, the war . . . He arrived here dead—" He added quickly, "As good as dead. Unknown, unwanted. Illegal. I took pity on him." He adjusted his ruby cuff links.

"He worked for you," Emily said.

"Odd jobs," Salwen said.

"Like getting names off tombstones?" Emily said.

"Be careful your reach doesn't exceed your grasp," Salwen snapped, pressing one finger directly down on the back of her hand.

"Who killed him?" Emily asked again, a-mazed she could keep her voice even.

He removed his finger and held up a hand to her. There was a spot of red on it. Her eyes flicked away from it.

"Ketchup, not blood," Salwen said, with a grin.

"Everything's a joke to you, isn't it?" she said, despising him. "Bringing in Nazis or collaborators disguised as Jews . . . it's such a hilarious idea. Who else would have thought of that but you? Who has that kind of humor? Jew killers into Jews! Side-splitting."

The waiter arrived with the food and set it reverently in front of her. She did not touch it.

"Eat," Salwen said. "Before it gets cold."

Emily pushed it away.

He sighed again, dramatically. He was enjoying himself. "You think the war is over," he said. He shook his head in an exaggerated motion from side to side. A gentleman in a tuxedo with an extremely beautiful woman who looked like a model stopped at Salwen's banquette to say hello. When they'd left, Salwen went on. "World War Two is over, sure. But World War Three? No. Batters up!"

There was a flurry of movement at the door and he looked up. Senator Byington and his wife had just entered and were being shown to a table. They were a handsome, sought-after, popular pair.

"Behold the sun . . . rising in the west," Salwen murmured. He watched the Byingtons as they paused to be greeted along the way, shaking hands, exchanging pleasantries and laughter. Emily watched Salwen's jaded, slightly bored expression shift to one of admiration for Senator Byington.

"Tomorrow he goes on the television," Salwen said, not taking his eyes from the Byingtons. "You should catch his appearance. The sincerity alone is a ticket to the White House. You want to invite him right into your living room." He glanced at her. "Excuse me, I forgot. You have the set in your bedroom."

"I'd like to go home," Emily said, a statement of fact, not a request.

"We haven't heard your part of the deal," he said, his hands embracing each other.

"You haven't told me about the boy," she said.

With great sincerity, Salwen said, "Why, you killed him, Emily. With the best of intentions, of course. You killed him with kindness. You're a do-gooder. Your hand goes out in charity—what does it matter if a boy falls by the wayside? He'd be alive if it wasn't for you." His eyes were riveted to her face.

You bastard, she thought, stung. She knew this partial truth was all she was going to get out of him. She had been a fool to try.

"Nobody else knows," Emily said, her voice low.

Salwen considered this and then nodded shortly. He looked up. Binney, one of his well-dressed aides, stood by the captain's station. Binney caught Salwen's eye, nodded, then turned and left. Salwen refocused on Emily.

"There's a car waiting to take you home," he said pleasantly. "Pity about your dinner."

"I can get home by myself," Emily said, getting to her feet. She didn't trust him for a min-

ute. "I'd rather take my chances on the street."
She tossed her napkin on the table.

When the cab dropped her in front of her
building, Emily looked up and down the street. It
was dark and deserted. She looked up at the
glass and oak door with the two marble columns
beside it. Had the front door always been so
dark? Or was she just noticing things like that
now? She felt as if she stood on a volcano. She
hurried up to the front door, pressed her key in
the lock, and scurried inside. She knew what
was really different; she no longer felt safe.
Ever.

Inside, she started up the stairs to her apartment, glancing up at the landing. She stopped.
The second-floor light was out. Instantly, she
felt the house surrounding her, silent and ominous, waiting. She turned, but going back out
the front door seemed more dangerous than
trying to reach her apartment.

Very slowly, feeling the sweat beading on her
forehead and running down her back, she
climbed the stairs to her door. Her hand was
shaking so much that she could hardly get the
key in the lock. Finally, ready to scream from
the tension, she flung the door open and rushed
inside.

It was dark and shadowy. Emily kicked the
door closed and reached for a light. Her hand
froze. Someone was in the apartment. She knew
it. Had she heard something? She waited, holding her breath, her hand still outstretched for

the wall switch. The silence had a menacing palpability to it.

Her heart was about to fly out of her chest. Carefully, she slipped out of her loafers, picked up the poker, and crept to the open archway that led into the tiny kitchen.

Cochran sat on the floor by the window in a pool of light from a street lamp outside. He was working on a small, round, metal object that lay on the floor in front of him. Liberty was sitting beside him, watching.

Emily collapsed in a chair and let the poker fall with a clank on the floor.

"It's a bomb," he said conversationally. "They had it wired to the stove. Would have gone up the first time you boiled water. I got it out of there, but that's as far as I—damn." He renewed his quiet concentration on the bomb.

Emily's eyes flew wide open. She started to speak but no words came out. She breathed in deeply and tried again. "Shouldn't we leave this place?" she whispered, her voice hoarse with terror.

Utterly focused on the bomb, Cochran said, "Let's see . . . these babies go off about a minute after you detach them and I've used half of that. So we've still got thirty seconds. You want to start counting?"

Emily started to count. "One . . . two . . . three . . . four . . ."

"I never was any good at bomb disposal."

"Now you tell me," she whispered. "Eight . . . nine . . ."

"Almost flunked the course. It's like doing a crossword puzzle. I could never do those, either. Shit," Cochran said.

"What's wrong?" she cried, frantic.

"Keep counting! I think I cut the wrong wire," Cochran said.

"Sixteen . . . seventeen," Emily said.

"Sorry about the language," Cochran said.

"That's okay," Emily said. She felt hysterical. "Don't think twice about it. Twenty-two, twenty-three. Cochran, can we get out of here?" she pleaded urgently. She glanced at Liberty, who was stretching lazily.

"I hate confessing defeat," he said.

"Twenty-six, twenty-seven—" Emily continued.

"Let's go!" Cochran yelled.

He leaped to his feet, scaring Liberty who flew backward out of Emily's reach. "Liberty!" she screamed. She rushed to the cat who darted out between her legs, thoroughly panicked. Cochran scooped her up as Emily started for the door. He grabbed her. "This way!" he said, pulling her to an open window and the fire escape. They climbed quickly out, clambered down to the floor below and huddled against the wall, waiting. Liberty dug her claws into Cochran's shoulder. Emily was still counting. "Thirty-eight, thirty-nine . . . Don't let her get away, Cochran, or it's finished."

"It should have gone off," Cochran said, wondering. "Maybe I cut the right wire."

A tremendous explosion rocked the side of the

building and the window of Emily's apartment blew out in a shimmering hail of glass. Cochran seized her shoulder and held her against the outside wall, using his body to protect her from the rain of glass and plaster. Her face scraped by the rough brick, the earth-shattering din filling her ears, Emily cried out softly.

Chapter 13

"But where are we, Cochran? I can't follow all those streets, I've never even seen some of those streets—" Emily knew she was skating on the edge of hysteria, but the words kept tumbling out of her like water out of a fountain. She felt like they'd been in a car for hours.

First, they had driven to Marilyn's apartment and dropped off Liberty.

"What are you doing loose on the streets?" Marilyn had asked, annoyed. "You look a sight! Why aren't you staying here?"

"I will now," Emily had said. "They just blew up my apartment. Aren't you lucky we saved Liberty?" She had dropped into a chair. "I've got a friend waiting. Could I borrow a dress?"

After Marilyn's, they drove south and west, ending up in what looked like a warehouse district. Emily shifted from one foot to another in the dim hallway. Cochran was fighting some keys to open a door. "What is this place, Cochran?" It was somewhere below Canal Street, unchartered territory for her.

"A place you'll be safe," Cochran said.

He thrust the door open. "I'll go first," he said. He led her through a two empty offices that smelled of oil, papers, and darkness.

"What are we going to do? Who are we going to tell about this? The president? 'Dear Mr. President . . . your government is bringing in war criminals. There is this lovely town in Connecticut filling up with them. Some are going on to Chicago. Please advise. Sincerely yours, Emily Crane.'"

"'P.S. Murder is part of the deal,'" Cochran added. He walked into a third office and turned on the lights.

"He knew he was going to kill me, Cochran. While he was ordering me dinner, the famous hamburger. He was only waiting to know who I'd told. It was the strangest, most appalling feeling." She looked around the office but went right on talking. "What would they have said, a gas leak? Smoking in bed?"

The room had no office furniture in it. Instead, it was full of surveillance equipment. A high-power telescope and a camera with a long lens stood side by side, pointing through a window at a building across the street. On the other side of the camera, on a table, were two tape recorders. They were very new and glistened in the light. A rumpled bed, recently slept in, was against one wall. In the other corner, a round table with drop leaves was flanked by a couple of wooden chairs. The room was muggy and stale. Outside, the heavy air threatened a summer rainstorm.

Emily's mouth was open. "You bring me

here?" she said, stunned. "This room is obviously used for only one purpose: to spy on somebody!"

"I knew you'd be safe here," Cochran said with a trace of apology. He went to the bed and examined it critically. "I better change these sheets."

He went to a closet and pulled out two sheets. He tugged the used sheets from the bed and began making it up. Emily sat down in one of the wooden chairs at the table.

"What am I going to do with you?" she asked, shaking her head. "Where do you always come from? This isn't your job, saving my life. What are you really? Are you real?"

He worked on the bed, folding the corners of the sheet carefully and lifting the mattress to hold them fast. "I'm real," he said, not looking at her.

"I wouldn't be alive if it weren't for you," Emily said, putting her feet up on the other straight chair.

"I also make a great hospital corner," he said. "See?"

Emily ignored his hospital corners. "That boy wouldn't be dead if it weren't for me," she said seriously.

He stopped working and looked up. "You didn't kill him," he said quietly.

"I played with his life. And yours and Alan's and Marilyn's, too, in a way, though they're not in any danger. But Miss Venable is. I told her a lot. I told people to trust me and I hurt them," Emily said. She looked pale. Her blond hair fell over half her face and she made no motion to push it away.

"You did what was right," Cochran reassured her.

"For *who*? Who did I do it for? For them or for me?" she said from her heart.

Gently but firmly, Cochran said, "We do what we think is right. That's all anyone can do. Sometimes people get hurt, like the kid. It wasn't your fault."

"Comforting Cochran," she said to the floor. "Nick-of-time Cochran, my lifesaver." She looked up at him. He was standing on the far side of the bed, smoothing down the sheet. He looked at her now and again, his piercing blue eyes stabbing her with concern. He was really very muscular, she thought, watching him pick up a third of the mattress with ease and slip the sheet under it. She could see the muscles moving under his white shirt. She hadn't seen him with his jacket off before. He'd rolled up his sleeves. He had a narrow waist. There was something touching and generous about his making up her bed.

Years later, when she looked back on this moment, she would know she was attracted to the strength and protection he could give her at one of the most frightening times in her life. And Mike Cochran was a very handsome man. But it was more than that, and less, too, because her attraction to Mike Cochran was many-layered. Being alone with him in a room some-where below Canal Street was romantic and intriguing. More than that, she didn't wholly trust him, she wasn't sure what his role was in the tangle of events that had engulfed her, yet she was and always had been attracted by risk.

"I think I'm falling in love with you," Emily said.

Cochran stopped making up the bed and smiled. A whisper of surprise floated over his face. "I think you're a little hysterical." He went back to his task, and when he'd finished, he sat down on the bed, bounced, rose, and poked it experimentally.

"There's been a lot of heavy agents sleeping on this, so it's a little soft, but I guess it'll do," he declared gently. She'd changed into a pale blue dress at Marilyn's house, one that had little straps that tied over her shoulders, holding the gathered bodice up. It was one of the prettiest dresses he'd seen on her.

"Are you going home?" Emily asked.

They looked at each other across the room. It was a freighted moment they had both known was coming.

"Do you want me to?" he asked.

She ducked her head. "Boys shouldn't ask. I was always told that. They should just make their move. Personally, I think asking is in order," she said.

"I never asked before," Cochran said. "But I think you are—very important to me."

"Are you asking now?"

He went to her and lifted her out of the chair. "Is this gratitude?" he asked.

She thought about it. "Oh, no," she said. They stared at each other. "But are you asking?"

"Yes. Yes I am."

Gazing at her, he slipped his arms around her waist and drew her to him. She felt his hand come up and cup the back of her head beneath her hair as his lips found hers. The kiss was very gentle but to Emily it felt like a collision. A fan of desire opened inside her. She clung to him, trembling.

They broke from the kiss with a gasp. He was, she saw, as moved as she. "I've wanted to do that for days," he whispered. Emily knew as she reached up to kiss him again that she was not going to deny herself the explosion of sensations she felt for him.

The second kiss drained her of strength yet swelled her excitement. Her legs felt rubbery, disconnected. Her ears rang. Mike swept an arm around her waist. "Come with me now," he said.

She sat down on the bed. He untied one of the thin straps at her shoulder. His hand was shaking, but his eyes never left her face. He untied the other and the dress fell open to her waist.

She was one of the most beautiful women he'd ever been with, but she was a great deal more than that to him. Her soft palm flattened against the side of his face, pulling him down into another kiss. He felt her quivering, his body was on fire for her, yet he did not want to hurry.

He kissed her eyes and her throat and sent tremors through her body. They lay back together. Anticipation flooded her. And later, naked beside his nakedness, he was persuasively gentle and passionate. She tugged at his chin, bringing his lips to hers. It was breathtaking to be so close to him, to be touching his waist and thighs and back and hair. She felt his tongue reach into her mouth and she shivered, her chest tightening. She was drowning in the sensations his long kisses exploded around her, inside her. And later still, locked together, she rode wave after wave of delicious heat with him, her excitement rising, receding, sailing, and spinning. He never let her go.

Chapter 14

Emily came awake gradually, dreamily conscious of the warm, solid body next to her. Her eyes focused on a blank wall. Where was she? She felt suspended in doubt, in a place where there was no time and no memory—only the walls and the friendly anonymous body next to her.

A series of clicks and soft whirring sounds popped into the room. She looked toward the sounds and saw the huge tape recorder reels automatically switching over. She remembered.

She looked at the sleeping Mike Cochran next to her. This August day was already hot, and she knew she was in love with him. She looked at his firm jaw, shadowed with whiskers, the faint movement of his full lips in sleep. Her eyes swept over his brow, across his eyes, down his temple. He had saved her life—twice—but he had also followed her persistently, he had spied on her, and he'd always conveniently been around to "save" her. She was not so foolish to believe that Mike Cochran had switched to her fundamental beliefs, nor was she sure that he hadn't been following her for other reasons than those that appeared on the surface. Perhaps the FBI, too, supported illegal refugees and helped protect them.

But for this moment, she deliberately shelved her doubts. Careful not to disturb him, she slipped out of bed. His shirt lay on the floor; she slipped it on and wandered to the window. It was a bright sunny day. She looked at the camera, then at the huge telescope next to it. She was tempted to use it, but she felt she shouldn't. She examined it, walking from one side to the other. She looked out the window, then finally bent down and squinted through the telescope.

She was immediately inside the room across the street where two people were just sitting down to breakfast.

"Hard to resist, isn't it?" Cochran said.

She jumped away from it.

"But I felt sneaky," she said. He was sitting up in bed.

"Good morning," he said, his voice rumbling in his chest.

"Good morning."

"Sorry I don't have a bathrobe," Cochran apologized.

"This is fine," she assured him shyly. She felt modestly unclothed before him in the morning light and pulled the shirt a little closer around her.

"Want some breakfast?" Cochran asked. "There's a luncheonette around the corner."

"No, thanks," Emily said. She pointed out the

window. "Who are you spying on?" she asked him.

"We call it investigating," he said dryly. He shrugged. "I don't know who they are. That's the truth. I'm not on this detail, I just borrowed the key." He drew his knees up underneath the sheet, clasped his arms around them, and gazed at her. "Do we have to talk about that?"

"No," Emily said.

After a moment, Cochran said, "You make sounds when you sleep."

"I know," she said.

"Little sounds. You can hardly hear them," Cochran said.

"Like a chipmunk," Emily said with a smile.

"I wouldn't go that far—" he said, smiling back.

"That's what my baby-sitter said. Well, she was more like a nanny, in ways. I'd get so embarrassed I wouldn't want to go to sleep," Emily said.

"You had a nanny?" he asked. "Where'd you live—England?"

"Not really a nanny—she came in after preschool. Edna Calhoun," she said. Edna had been warm and she'd smelled of talcum powder and sugar. Her cheeks were always pink, and her hands soft, like her voice. "She used to read to me all the time. That's how I came to love books. And she'd tell me stories and talk to me. Except for my brother, nobody talked to me . . . in my family."

"You liked her," Cochran said.

Emily nodded, "My mother sent her away when I was eight. She thought we were getting too close." That awful moment came back like a slap—coming home from school with Jeff and calling for Edna because Emily had just been given a 100 percent in spelling. She'd wanted to tell Edna and watch the smile curl along her pink lips. But Edna wasn't there. Edna was never there again.

"That must have been rough," Cochran said sympathetically.

"Mother really thought I loved Edna more than I loved her. Maybe I did," Emily said.

He reached out his hand and she went to him and sat on the edge of the bed.

"Maybe you weren't so privileged," he said. He kissed her gently.

"You're tender, Cochran. That's what did it," she said softly.

Cochran kissed her again. "Why don't we just pull down the shades and come back to bed?" he said.

Between kisses, Emily said, "We can't."

"Why not?" he asked.

"There aren't any shades," Emily said, laughing. She kissed the matted hair on his chest.

"Oh. Well, we could put a blanket over the window," Cochran said.

Emily shook her head, serious now. "They're not going to let us alone, Cochran."

"First they have to find us," Cochran said.

He wanted to kiss her again, but she stood up and moved away.

"They won't have to find us," Emily said briskly. "We'll go to them. That's who we are, Cochran. We're believers."

"What does that mean?" he asked.

She was standing by the telescope. "But we believe different things." She turned the telescope on him. "You'll always be looking at me through this," she said.

"I don't think of us that way," he said.

"You have to. We're oil and water . . . patriots on opposite sides," she said, wistfully. "You're already enrolled in World War Three. But I don't accept that. We may be lovers, but we're enemies, too."

"Not last night, we weren't," he said.

Emily touched the telescope. "In the dark, this disappeared. But it's morning now." She went over to him. "Cochran, darling Cochran . . . Why couldn't we have met in World War Two?"

He hesitated, stroking her hair. "I hated New York until I met you."

They kissed again, holding each other, and then he swung briskly out of bed.

"Well . . . lose the horse, lose the buggy," he said. She looked at him, puzzled. "Game plan one: we try to stop them, don't we?" She nodded. "Well! They're leaving today. By tomorrow, they'll have new names. They'll disappear."

"You can't. You've been warned off. They catch you again, you know what can happen," Emily warned.

"Don't confuse me," he said.

"Cochran, why are you doing all this?" Emily asked.

"Don't you get tired of asking that question?" he said.

"Are you doing this for me?" she asked, hoping for an answer. When none came, she said again, "We're not on the same side."

"That's the big picture. Right now, let's think small," he said.

"Don't joke," Emily said.

"Don't ask me why," Cochran said. "I don't know why I'm doing this. Well, I do and I don't. I'm confused. All right?"

"I don't think you're confused," Emily said.

"You don't know me very well. I confuse easily. Ask anyone."

He pulled on his trousers and began putting keys and coins into the pockets.

"Put the other floodlight over there, right there," a photographer directed one of his assistants. They were lighting a photo session for *LOOK*. Warren Barringer stood on the sidelines, watching glumly. "Where is he? May we have the senator, please?" the photographer called out, checking his watch. Senator Byington's aide bounced into the pool of bright light.

"Will I do for the moment? You want someone for lights?"

"Yes," said the photographer. "Just sit here," he directed the aide.

Warren bent down to catch the words of his assistant. "What?" he asked, bored. "I didn't hear you." The assistant whispered in his ear, harsh sibilants. Warren's eyes widened, and he felt a shiver of fear. He spun around to see Emily and Cochran standing by the front door. Emily was waving cheerily at him. Warren ground his teeth unconsciously, wanting to avoid her. But there was no way. He looked nervously indecisive, hesitated, then surrendered and walked over to them.

"Hi, Warren. Buy any more pocketbooks lately?" Emily said with a big smile.

"Emily, we don't want trouble—" Warren said.

"No trouble, Warren. We just want to see Senator Byington. I hear you're doing a cover on him," she said.

"I'm sorry, Emily. That's out of the question," Warren said.

"I'll tell you what, Warren," Emily said, letting her smile fade and staring at him with ice in her eyes. "If you don't take us to see Senator Byington, I'm going to tell everybody you're a communist."

Warren sucked in his breath. "That's a cheap stupid trick, Emily. It won't work." But he knew she meant it.

"In this climate? I'm going to say you chose pictures that showed America in the worst possible light, and you know what? They'll believe me!" She forced a laugh that sounded almost natural. "It's a cockamamie world, Warren." She cocked her head toward Mike. "This is Mr. Cochran. He's from the FBI," Emily said. "I've told him everything."

"What! It's not true!" Warren exclaimed.

"Prove it," Emily said sweetly.

"No one will believe you," Warren hissed, looking at Cochran.

"Now, now, Warren, *everyone* will believe me," she said, dropping her smile. He glared at her.

"Hey, Emily!" the photographer called out. "How're you doing?"

Emily waved back. "Just fine, Dave! I love the way you've lit the flag." An assistant with a clipboard rushed past her and called out a greeting.

Warren turned sullenly and motioned for Emily and Cochran to follow him. A young woman with long auburn hair hurried up to Emily.

"Em! Does this mean you're back on the job?" she asked.

"Not yet, Annie," Emily said.

Disappointed, Annie said, "Oh. I thought for a minute . . ."

Emily nodded. "They'll come to their senses. Warren's working on it," Emily said as she headed toward the dressing rooms.

Byington sat before a mirrored makeup table ringed with light bulbs. He wore a towel as a bib across his jacket front.

"Senator," Warren began, "I'd like you to meet Miss Emily Crane, formerly of our offices, and, er—"

"Mike Cochran, FBI," he supplied.

Byington was mildly surprised, but he was a courteous man and the process of making up for the camera was not only boring but a trifle degrading. He welcomed the diversion.

Emily launched into the reason they were there, starting from the moment she appeared before the committee. "Yes," said Byington, "you did look familiar, but there are so many—"

"And then I was fired," she said, glancing at Warren, enjoying his discomfort. She went straight through the events at the Carroll Street house, the murder of Stefan, the wedding, and the discovery of the illegal aliens, whom she labeled as former Nazis. "At the very least," she said, "they were Nazi collaborators during the Ukrainian occupation. They are certainly over here with a German, Dr. Teperson, and if you check, I think you'll find he's a Nazi."

"Why come to me?" Byington asked suspiciously.

"I wouldn't have if I'd just known you from the hearings. But I heard you speak on Boyle's television show. You talked about not losing the peace, about what we fought for," Emily said passionately. "These men are what we fought *against*."

"You're sure they're war criminals?" Byington asked.

"They're being smuggled in!" Emily cried.

"But you don't really know who they are," Byington said.

"Not their real names, we haven't had time. We're trying to find out," Cochran said.

"And you claim Sam Salwen is behind all this?" Byington asked Emily. He sounded very dubious.

"I *know* he is," Emily declared without hesitation.

"You have evidence?" Byington asked.

"Yes," Emily lied.

Byington turned away from them and gazed into the mirror thoughtfully. Finally he said, "You hear this kind of thing is going on, but you can't pin it down. They don't tell Congress. They don't even tell the State Department. They think they have some kind of license called patriotism." Byington shook his head. "The boy who was murdered . . . I can't do anything about him. That's for the police. But the rest of them . . . Sam Salwen . . . I will do something about him." The senator held out his hand. "Thanks for bringing this to me, I appreciate your trust."

They shook hands with him and left. Emily felt buoyed up. Byington could hear her saying good-bye to her friends as they left the studio.

He sat quietly for a long moment, waiting for the door behind him to open. When it did, Byington did not look up. He knew it was Salwen.

"You didn't tell me about *this* group," Byington said.

Chapter 15

"What's to tell?" Salwen said, spreading his hands out. "A favor for important people in Defense."

"But I certified they were genuine refugees!" Byington snapped, clearly upset by Sam's deception.

"They're a hundred percent genuine," Salwen assured him. "Direct from the old country."

But Byington wasn't letting go of it. "What are they, Sam? Scientists for the rocket program?"

"There's none of them left. What we didn't get, the Russians got," Salwen said. "These are doctors."

"What kind of doctors?" Byington asked.

"Research, that's all. Air-force research."

"But what kind of research?" Byington pressed on angrily. "Where?"

"I know what you're worried about," Salwen said with an edge in his voice. "But rest assured. These people were only technicians."

"Meaning?" Byington said.

"Test tubes! Blood samples!" Salwen straightened his jacket and glared at Byington. "You think I didn't make sure? These men are clean, I tell you. They were working with Teperson, they knew his procedures."

"Then why the secrecy? The false names?"

"They are technicians in a sensitive area. Vital to national security. It's as simple as that," Salwen assured him. He'd regained his composure. His tone was sincere and convincing.

Byington looked at him searchingly. "I've trusted you, Sam," the senator said quietly.

"Would I abuse that trust? There is nothing here that will harm your reputation," Salwen said.

"We're not talking about my reputation!" Byington declared.

"We're talking about a presidential hopeful. A man the whole country is taking to its heart." Salwen knew Byington. The senator wouldn't admit it, but he was damn sure worried about the flap medical technicians from concentration camps could cause if it got out that the senator's office helped bring them to the States. Salwen also knew that Byington was going through the motions. He wouldn't press much further. "You have a noble ambition, Senator. That's why I'm here—to help you reach the pinnacle. This other thing . . . really, it's just a small favor of small importance," Salwen finished, dismissing it.

"If these men are war criminals—" Byington began.

"I assure you they are not!" Salwen said, exasperated.

Byington was silent. He still wasn't completely convinced but he'd pressed Salwen as hard as he could. He'd get no further information from him.

Salwen was looking at him critically. "They put too much makeup on you. You've got an outdoor complexion so you don't need that much. Detracts from your virility." Salwen took a tissue from a box and started gently wiping Byington's face.

The senator took the tissue from him. "Leave it, Sam. Just leave it."

Back in the surveillance room, which had been the curious setting for their passionate interlude of the night before, Cochran said to Emily, "Stay in this room, okay? Until I call. There are very nasty people out there."

"I still think we should go to Grand Central, watch the train to Chicago, and make sure that Byington's on top of this," Emily said. "We can't let them get away."

"If he does what he says," Cochran explained patiently, "that won't be necessary. If he doesn't, it won't be possible." He went to the equipment and started changing reels.

"You don't know until you try," Emily said.

"Do you want to quit?" Cochran asked.

"No!" She turned away. "Their train leaves at six," she added.

He finished changing the reels, putting the ones that had been exposed into a large manila envelope. "I will call you by three o'clock. That's plenty of time, okay? Meanwhile, you do not leave this room. This isn't over yet," Cochran said, running a hand along her cheek.

"What if someone comes up here?"

"They won't. But don't open the door if they do." She looked worried, but he knew it was because she had to wait, and waiting was the hard part. He kissed her, and reluctantly started for the door. Then he turned. "Emily," he said with great tenderness. He returned and embraced her, breathing in the scent of her hair and feeling the soft curves of her body. "Oh, Emily," he said. She had become very dear to him. "Double-lock the door," he whispered, slowly breaking away from her.

A few blocks down from the big FBI building in midtown Manhattan, Cochran was bending over the desk of a clerk in the offices of the U.S. Immigration Service. He'd done a lot of fast talking, and he'd flashed his FBI identification badge, as well as his smile. The clerk was a young woman, new on the job, and she wasn't sure what the procedure was. Her large brown eyes looked worried.

"Mr. Cochran, I—I guess this is okay, but it's, I mean, I think it's irregular—" She was rising from her desk. "Follow me."

"You just call downtown if you want, but I can assure you that Agent Hackett will be here in approximately five minutes."

"Okay, okay, but I gotta check with my boss when he gets back from lunch," she said, pulling at her bouffant skirt. "This way."

Cochran checked his watch. It was after one o'clock. He could imagine how nervous Emily would be.

"Mr. Morse," said the clerk, "this is Mr. Cochran from the FBI. He needs to look into some files."

"What can I do for you, Mr. Cochran?" asked Morse. He was a plump man who liked to get along. Morse was in charge of the Immigration Services library system.

"We've got a tip and not much time to work on it," said Cochran, giving him enough information to get the ball rolling, but not enough to excite his insecurities. "The tip is that some war criminals have entered the U.S. illegally, seeking new identities. I need to see some of your slides."

Morse opened the door of a darkened room—a vast file room of the immigration 140 service. He went to one of the huge numbered containers, indicated a chair for Cochran, and started leafing through a book on top of the file cabinet. "Pretty tall order," he said, wheezing a bit. He sneezed. "Damn it! Hay fever. Gets me every year about this time."

"Rough," said Cochran, trying not to be impatient.

Sniffing noisily, Morse withdrew a carousel of slides, rechecked his book, then turned on the slide projector. "You got any idea what grade these guys are?"

"Nope. Only that they've worked in the camps, and that—well, it's a long story, Morse, but I'll recognize them when I see them."

"But we got hundreds here." Morse looked at Cochran, astonished.

"Try the camps where we know most of the inmates were Russian or Ukrainian."

Morse huffed and sneezed again. "That doesn't narrow it a whole lot." He was beginning to feel put upon. He inserted the slide carousel and flicked a switch. Up on a screen, a grainy picture of a Nazi officer taken during World War II appeared.

"You can really rip through them," said Cochran, knowing how much of a long shot he was playing.

They went through three carousels, snapping off the shots. Cochran was slumped in a chair, weary and discouraged. He shook his head.

"Uh-uh . . ." Cochran said. He checked his watch. "Wait," he said, then, "No, sorry." The pictures continued; the faces blurred.

In the surveillance room, Emily was pacing back and forth, checking her watch every minute. She looked through the telescope, but the apartment across the street was empty. When she needed some illegal and immoral diversion, where was it?

She remembered her mother and sprang to the telephone. Her mother was coming over to her apartment for lunch, and her apartment wasn't even there anymore! Emily rang the Dworkins.

Marilyn was furious. "Where are you?" she demanded. "Your mother is a basket case! We all are!"

"The FBI is hiding me out," Emily said, trying to sound calm. "Tell Mom I'm very sorry—"

"Tell her yourself," Marilyn snapped.

Emily heard Marilyn shouting, and then her mother came on the line. "Oh, Emily, when I got to the building and saw that ghastly hole where your pretty little apartment had been—well—I thought I'd lost you. . . ." Mrs. Crane broke down, weeping.

In her whole life, Emily's mother had never cried for her. In fact, she'd never seen her express any emotion except on the day Jeff had died.

"I'm okay, Mother. I'm sorry . . ."

Mrs. Crane struggled against her unusual tears. "Now, honey, where are you? When are you coming here?"

"The FBI is keeping me under protective custody. I can't come back till tonight—"

"I'm not leaving this city, Emily Elizabeth, until I know you're all right," her mother declared, surrendering to her tears again.

Emily replaced the receiver and stared out the window. Slowly, she looked at her watch again. It was after three. "I don't care what he said," she muttered. "I'm not staying here another minute!" She threw on her jacket and charged out the door. She felt quite bucked up that her mother was so sad. Emily had never realized that her mother cared about her.

Cochran had seen so many slides that he didn't think he'd recognize his own mother if she popped up on the screen.

"This is the last box of this batch," Morse said, bored stiff. "And then I have to get back to my—"

"Hold it right there," Cochran said, sitting up.

Teperson—much younger, without a mustache—bounced up on the screen.

The phone rang and Morse edged his bulk out from behind the projector to pick it up. "Library . . . Morse speaking. Yessir . . . yes sir . . ." Morse hung up. "Cochran?"

"Yeah?"

"You're office wants you—in the director's office," Morse said with renewed respect.

"Don't you lose that slide," Cochran said, rising. "You do, and we've lost the war—you understand me?"

Grand Central Station, the railroad nerve center in the heart of Manhattan, streamed with travelers. Grand Central—and its sister station, Penn Station in the West Thirties—was only empty in the tiny, dead hours before dawn.

It was three-thirty in the afternoon. The Chicago Express, due to depart from the Lower Concourse Gate 111–112, was slowly backing under the housing of the platform, supervised by trainmen. A young gateman with carrot-red hair came through the gate, locking it behind him, and started putting up the notice for the express. Departure time: six that evening. Two husky men in caps were getting ready to roll out the red carpet. The gateman began putting up the rest of the Chicago Express's facilities on the board:

drawing rooms, compartments, roomettes, dining car, club car, barber shop.

Emily stood below the gateman. "Hey! Mister!" she called out, trying to get his attention. He didn't look at her. "Excuse me! Are my passengers on the train yet?"

"Gates don't open till five," the gateman said.

"Then nobody's on . . . I mean, no passengers," she said.

"Nope," he replied, not looking down.

"Thank you," Emily said.

"Unless they are some big shots," the gateman said as he turned away. "Movie stars. Politicians. Sometimes they get put on first."

Emily looked through the gate with renewed interest. The men were unrolling the red carpet.

"Damn," Cochran said to himself as he sprinted up the stairs at the FBI office. They were on to him already. He'd have to do some really fast backing and filling now, but he had his ace: Teperson, a.k.a. Colonel Hans Erlich, SS.

Cochran bounced past Patricia, the director's secretary, who looked at him and rolled her eyes. "Go right on in," she said, flipping the intercom switch.

Cochran knocked on the door anyway. "Come in," the director said in a sharp voice. Cochran entered.

Ron Balone, the director, was sitting behind his desk looking at a file that was stamped top secret. His slicked-back hair glistened with Brilliantine. His sharp eyes belied the laconic way he handled business. "Oh, Cochran," he said. "I've been looking for you. Sit down."

But Cochran was looking at the other man in the room. It was the man with the bushy black mustache who had steered Tom, Dick, and Harry through Immigration, and taken them on to the wedding.

"We've got a few things to talk about," the director said. "This is Paul Blake from Defense. Seems you've run afoul of their line."

Emily rushed upstairs to the main concourse and dove into a phone booth. She reached into her pocket, put a nickel in the slot, and dialed Cochran's desk at the FBI. It rang and rang.

Finally, a rough voice came on the line. "Agent Hackett," Hackett said.

"Is Cochran there?" Emily asked, grimacing. She didn't like Hackett and she didn't want to talk to him. "May I speak to him, please?"

"Who's this?"

She hesitated. "Emily Crane."

"He's in conference, Miss Crane," Hackett said.

"Please tell him I'm at Grand Central Station. Our people might be on the train already. Will you tell him that?"

"Miss Crane—" Hackett began, but Emily hung up.

Chapter 16

When Cochran came out of the director's office, Sid Hackett was waiting for him.

"She called. She's at Grand Central," Hackett said.

"That figures. Damn it," Cochran said.

Hackett hooked a stubby finger at the director's office. "What happened in there?"

"I'm off the case," Cochran said.

"What else?"

"I can't tell anyone what I know," Cochran said.

"That's all?" Hackett said.

"And I've got to stay away from her," Cochran added.

Before Hackett could say anything else, Cochran was out the door. "Damned idiot," Hackett mumbled, shaking his head. He was fond of Cochran, but Cochran was dealing himself right out of the Bureau.

At the Vanderbilt Avenue entrance to Grand Central's main concourse, the traffic was picking up. Rush hour was beginning, and people were heading home. Taxis and cars entered and left at a fast clip. A black limo slipped to the curb. Salwen got out. Binney and another aide were right behind him. As the limo nosed away, Salwen said to them, "No slip-ups. You got the IDs?" They nodded, and showed him their false papers identifying them as Immigration agents. Salwen felt triumphant. He had all but pulled off a tremendously difficult task. It would redound to his credit, among the tiny inner circle of government, for a generation. Or more, he said to himself. Or more.

Salwen moved to the head of the wide marble staircase that led to the concourse. "Shit," he said under his breath. "I don't believe it!" Emily Crane was heading toward the Chicago gate. "See that girl down there—the one with the blond hair?" Selwen asked his aides. Binney recognized her. "No way is she to get on that train, do you understand. I don't care what we have to do to prevent it."

Emily didn't see Salwen and his aides as she rushed back to the platform. The red carpet was unrolled and in place. Conductors were preparing a long table on the platform to check through passengers.

She sat down on a bench where she could see the gate, and opened a newspaper she'd bought. She checked her watch nervously. She got up and raced over to the ladies' room.

When she came out of a stall a few minutes later, she found herself at the large mirror with a bleached blond girl who was heavily outlining her lips in coral lipstick.

"Hiya!" the girl said. "Hey, can I—I wonder if you could let me use an eyeliner pencil. You got one?"

Emily dug around in her purse and found one for her. The girl chattered on, chewing gum with a quick rotating motion of her jaw. She bent close to the mirror to get her eyes right. When she mentioned she was the manicurist on the Twentieth Century to Chicago, Emily looked at her with real interest.

The gateman was unlocking the gate when the barber came up to it. He carried a shiny black leather bag.

"How you doing, Benny?" the barber said.

"Never mind that. How about the haircut you promised," Benny said.

"Next trip," the barber promised, going through the gate.

"That's what you said last trip," Benny said, and calling out after him, "A manicure, too!"

Two manicurists came after the barber.

"You're too old for a manicure, Benny," the first manicurist said. She pumped up her bleached blond hair with her hand.

"Not if you sit on my lap. Then you'll see how old I am," Benny said, leering at her.

"Talk, talk," the manicurist replied, swiveling her hips in the tight black skirt.

"Hiya," said the second manicurist, furiously chewing gum. Benny smiled at her. She was quite a dish. The manicurists followed the bar-

ber through the gate. The second one had a
rolling swing in her hips. Benny watched her for
a moment, then locked the gate again.

On the platform, the barber and the manicurists climbed onto the train and headed toward
the cars at the rear. Everyone was too busy with
their own work to notice Emily, the second
manicurist. Emily started forward. She passed
through the dining car, where the waiters were
setting up the tables, through the kitchen where
the chefs were preparing the food. Boxes of
fresh fish and cherry pies were being loaded on.
Out in the lounge, a tall black bartender was
polishing glasses. Everyone was friendly and
smiled at her. She went through with a wave. At
the first car of compartments she tentatively
tried a door; it was locked. She tried another; the
same.

"Help you, miss?" the porter asked, coming
toward her.

"I thought some friends of mine might have
boarded early," she said.

"Three men?" the porter said.

"Yes!" Emily replied.

"Government people?" he asked.

"Are they here?" Emily said.

The porter motioned with his head for her to
follow him.

"I just want to know if they're on board,"
Emily said quickly.

"Just keep a-coming," he said, with a smile.

He started back through the car. Emily followed.

In the vestibule between two cars the porter

said, "Got to go out and around. Locked up here." He took her arm. "Easy, now."

He helped her off the train. Still holding her arm, the porter called out, "This the one?"

Salwen and his aides stood by the gate. As they started forward, Emily struggled against the porter's grip, but his hand was like iron; he held her fast.

"Let me go! You don't know what you're doing!" she cried.

"You're on the Twentieth Century, miss. You can't go playing no tricks on the Century," the porter said.

A large hamper came by with linens for the train, and still holding Emily, the porter stepped aside to let it pass. But the move made him loosen his grip and she twisted away. Salwen's aides were advancing on her rapidly; they looked grim as death. She knew she'd never get past them, so she dashed toward the front of the platform. At the end, a flight of narrow, dingy steps led down onto the tracks. She ran past two startled train crewmen working on the engine and tore down the steps. They shouted after her as she disappeared into the train tunnel.

Oh, God, she thought, *what am I doing?* But she had to keep away from Salwen. He'd kill her this time. She was sure of it.

The tunnel, on a lower level, was dimly lit. A massive locomotive was moved slowly toward her. She ran to cross the track before it reached her, but she couldn't make it and had to pull back. The train stopped, blocking her escape route. She looked around. The two aides were silhouetted in the darkness on the stairs. They were moving toward her.

Emily went forward, picking her way, and rounded a corner. She could just make out the shape of a circular staircase ahead. She made a dash for it and started up, but stopped in terror. A dark shape blocked her exit at the top of the stairs. *How did they know?* Emily wondered, panicked. She turned around to run back, but the figure leaped down the stairs and seized her.

"Why can't you stay in one place?" Cochran asked.

"Cochran!" Emily said, half hysterical. "Why do you keep scaring me?" She leaned against him, thankful. He patted her shoulder, kissed her neck hurriedly, took hold of her hand. They made their way up the stairs and out a door.

"My God, can't you do anything?" Salwen demanded. Binney appeared unmoved, but he knew both he and the other aide were in for it when this was over. "How could you lose her? I ought to have *her* for my aide instead of—"

He was seething. They were standing on the balcony level overlooking the station's main concourse.

"There are a dozen doors down there. It's a labyrinth, Mr. Salwen. But they all lead back to the concourse or into the main yard. I've sent Jack into the yard to watch for her."

"Binney, you'll pay for this if she gets away. This operation is delicate enough—" His mouth snapped shut. He detested strong emotions. Besides, he had an ace up his sleeve.

Emily and Mike were in a back corridor that opened onto the concourse. Cochran stopped at the doorway and looked out. He turned back to Emily.

"I don't see anyone we know, but I don't want to take the chance. We'll go up and around," he said.

He led her to an elevator and pressed the up button. "God, how do you know your way around this place?" she asked. Her cheeks were pink from her run, and she was still panting.

"Grand Central one-oh-one," he said, "FBI school." He looked at her, annoyed. "I should have locked the door from the outside. I would have been here, Emily, right on top of it. But I wanted you out of it. They'll do anything—"

"Byington didn't do anything, Cochran," Emily said. "I guess he thought I was crazy or something. Those guys are going to be on this train."

The elevator came. Two workmen in overalls were on it and they eyed Cochran and Emily carefully. "Hello, fellas," said Cochran cheerily. He pressed the first-floor button and the door closed. The elevator rose jerkily.

Emily took Cochran's arm. "Mike, we ought to check the other corridor for that luggage, too, don't you think?" He looked at her, baffled. She smiled much too brightly and rolled her eyes at the men. The elevator stopped and the door opened.

McKay blocked all the light. He had a new knife and an old grudge. Emily screamed as McKay lunged at Cochran exactly as he had lunged at Stefan. It was like a nightmare repeated. But Cochran was no rabbit waiting for slaughter. He grabbed McKay's arm and yanked him into the elevator. The workmen lurched backward.

"Get out!" Cochran bellowed to Emily.

She jumped out as the elevator door closed behind her.

Inside, Cochran and McKay were locked in a close, savage battle. The workmen, shocked, flattened themselves against the sides of the elevator, trying to stay out of the way of the slicing and diving knife. Emily, outside, could hear the grotesque sounds inside the elevator, which was still arrested at the first floor. Mike was only a foot away from her, but what could she do? She glanced down the corridor: the two aides were coming toward her. She whirled and dashed the other way to a staircase and took the steps two at a time.

She reached the top of the stairs, went through the first door she saw and forced herself up another staircase. She burst out into another, narrower corridor.

About twenty yards away, the freight elevator opened and the two workmen backed out. Cochran, his jacket torn and his body bent in exhaustion, pulled McKay's body out of the elevator. Emily ran toward them. "Mike," she said, trying to shout, but she was so winded she could hardly speak. Cochran leaped back in the elevator.

Just as she reached it, the doors closed.
"Mike!"

"Upstairs," he said through the door. McKay
lay curled on the floor, dead, his hand still
clutching his knife. She shuddered.

She could hear the aides' footsteps, running on
marble floors. She raced down the hall, flung
open a door and started up a flight of stairs as
the aides were passing the elevator. She
rounded a bend on the stairs. In the middle of
the staircase she saw a door to her right. Afraid
of the aides, she plunged through it and came
out on a narrow ledge with such speed that she
nearly went sailing over it. She gripped the
doorjamb, horrified.

Far below Grand Central's main concourse
was filling up with people charging in every
direction. She flattened herself against the wall.
Primal terror seized her. She felt the pull of
vertigo, the seductive, screaming urge to step off
the ledge and fall, fall into space, surrendering.
She closed her eyes. Drops of perspiration rolled
down her forehead into her eye. She couldn't
wipe them away; if she moved her hand, she'd
lose her balance. She was panting from the
chase; each breath threatened to send her flying
off the ledge. Her eyelids were made of marble.
She forced them to open. "Be calm," she said to
herself. "Don't look down." But the malignant
desire to look down into death, to submit, drew
her into its orbit. She felt her head turning,
dropping. The concourse below was spinning. It
was a vortex. It was calling for her. It was sweet.
It held out its arms.

At the last minute, she pushed her head back and looked up at the ceiling of the vast station. It was a painted constellation of stars and sky. She had no idea how long she was frozen on the ledge, staring into the painted stars. Finally, she looked to the right; the ledge just ended. She looked to the left: a doorway fit into a large window. She inched her way along the ledge toward the doorway, toward safety, toward life.

From below, on the far balcony level, Salwen looked up at the clock and frowned. There was a tiny figure on a ledge high above the vast concourse. He narrowed his eyes. Was that someone standing up there Emily Crane? He thought it was. Below him, on the stairway leading down into the concourse, Matilde had joined Teperson and his three assistants from the boat, as well as Simpson. They came down the stairs and headed for the Twentieth Century gate.

On the ledge, Emily was halfway to the door built into the large window when it opened. One of the aides stepped through it. Emily stopped. She was trapped. The seductive whirlpool of height and space reached out for her again. The aide stepped onto the ledge. He was agile. Sweating, terrified, she stiffly reversed herself, going back, one step, another, a third. She made for the first doorway and stepped through it. She banged it shut and locked it by turning the bolt. She collapsed on the top step, her ears ringing. She was going to faint.

"No!" she wailed. "No! I don't want to die." The aide was pushing at the door. Her body weighed a thousand pounds. She hiked herself up and swayed against the wall. Then she staggered down the steps, onto the main staircase, and climbed two flights to a door at the top. She pressed it open and gasped.

She was facing a narrow walkway that spanned the roof. A huge flat cement surface, the false ceiling of the main concourse, stretched about twenty feet below the catwalk. There were two doors—hers and one at the other end. It seemed as far away as a football field.

She could not stay where she was. She concentrated on the door at the far end and started along the catwalk. The door opened: Salwen! He was smiling at her.

"You know, none of this had to happen," he said across the empty space. He advanced on her; she backed away. "None of it. Why couldn't you just stop? What was so important? A boy from nowhere? I refuse to believe that."

Emily jumped from the catwalk to a narrow beam and slipped. Her foot touched the plaster and rabbit wire of the false ceiling. There was a cracking sound. She quickly regained her footing on the beam. "That's not safe," he said, a satisfied smile on his lips. "Just wait there and we'll both get down." Emily wasn't having any of that. She was safer putting her one hundred and ten pounds on a false ceiling and hoping the rabbit wire would hold than waiting for him to reach her.

"What was so important?" Salwen intoned again as he approached. "Those Nazis? Who cares about them anymore? They're the wave of the past. In ten years, twenty, they'll be a foot-note of history."

A small crack appeared at the edge of the false roof. Dust and plaster floated down.

Emily had come to a stop against the ironwork that led to the windows and the upper roof.

"You keep looking backward, Emily. You don't look to the future. Look at *me*, Emily," Salwen ordered in a creamy voice full of malevolence.

But Emily was looking up at an open window above her. If she looked down, she knew she would surrender, let go of this last handhold on life.

"There's still time," Salwen said, changing his tone seductively. "We can go somewhere, talk this over . . . bury the hatchet. Believe me, we can live and let live. It was never personal with me. It never is."

He was almost on her when she started climbing up toward the window. "Don't give up," she kept repeating to herself. Salwen reached for her leg, and missed. She kicked back at him, but he seized her leg and pulled at her. "Let go!" she cried. She felt her fingers slipping from the fragile hold she had on the ornate windowsill. She crashed against him, knocking him off the catwalk. Frantic, she clutched at the ironwork, swayed for a moment, but kept her balance.

She looked down. Salwen was spread-eagled on the plaster and rabbit wire. He looked dazed. Then he began to move, pulling himself up. "Don't," she said, hearing the plaster begin to crack beneath him. He looked up at Emily, their eyes met, and then a sound like a timber cracking split the air and he hurtled through the ceiling.

From the other side inside the station, Binney was standing on the balcony looking for Salwen. He heard the ominous but curiously smothered cracking sound, glanced up, and saw Salwen's body breaking through the roof. Salwen was screaming as he hurtled to the floor below. Binney crossed himself, frozen with horror.

On the mezzanine, Cochran looked up into the hole in the ceiling. Emily stood on a beam, clutching something out of sight, looking down. He could feel her terror like a sweat as he made for the stairs.

An hour later, on the platform of gate 112, a conductor stood by an open door of the Twentieth Century. A lantern waved at the head of the train.

"Boaaarrrd!" the conductor roared. Last-minute passengers raced to the nearest doors, and collided with people trying to get off. The conductor gave one last call, hoisted his footstool, and climbed on the train as it started.

In the club car, a porter brought drinks for four men and a woman. "Here you are," the porter said, putting the drinks down in front of them. The woman exchanged a smile with a tall man whose hair was white. The happy group raised their glasses in a toast. They spoke a foreign language. *Refugees*, the porter thought. *Well, let 'em enjoy their newfound freedom.* That's the way the porter liked to see his passengers when they were starting out. Laughing. Talking.

He turned to welcome a young couple into the car. But when he got up close, their appearance shocked him. The woman's dress was torn and dirty, her hair disheveled; the man's trousers looked as though he'd slept in them on the tracks. "Can I help you?" he asked dubiously. Compared to the other passengers, they looked like bums. They didn't belong in his club car.

"We're just joining some friends," Emily said. She advanced on the ebullient group at the far end of his car.

"Just a minute," said the porter. Simpson looked up and saw them. The train went into a tunnel. Simpson rose, holding on to the table in the dark, but he managed to seize Cochran's arm.

"Get out of here. I'm giving you a break," Simpson warned Cochran in a low voice. The train came out of the tunnel.

"You have no right—" Matilde yelled.

"Watch me," Cochran said as he pointed to the men, "You, you, you, and you. You're under arrest."

"Cochran, you're crazy," Simpson said.

Cochran nodded. "That's right. I just killed a guy. I'm not myself." To the men, he said, "Keep your hands on the table. I want you safe for trial."

"Don't be ridiculous," Matilde said, a note of forced outrage creeping into her voice. "These men are legitimate refugees. They have papers."

"Sackadorf. Hurwitz. Bistrong," Cochran said, pointing to them as he said their names.

"Exactly," Matilde said.

"And Teperson," Cochran said, pointing to the fourth.

He took a piece of paper from his pocket.

"Don't mess with this," Simpson said through his teeth. "You're not going to get anywhere—"

Reading, Cochran said, "Real name: Antulovich, Pavel. In charge of experiments in how long a man can survive in ice water before he freezes to death. Subject of experiments? Prisoners in Auschwitz." He turned to the woman. "You want others? How about the one that involved suffocation—how long people can live without air."

"I wouldn't want to be you, Cochran," Simpson said. "You know what they're going to do to you?"

"Maybe they'll give him a medal," Emily piped up. "He deserves a medal." She reached up and pulled the emergency cord with all her might. The train screeched violently. The impact of the locked wheels threw everyone not hanging on to their seats to the floor.

Emily was sorry for the porter, who was carrying a tray of whiskey sours; otherwise, she felt just fine.

Chapter 17

"I am not interested in Nazis *or* the FBI," snapped Mrs. Crane. "What do they have to do with real life? I want you to come home with me. Now." Her mother was wearing a flowered house coat and a small silver bracelet. She had no makeup on her face and Emily could see that in not too many years she might look as old as Miss Venable.

Emily, her mother, and Marilyn were sitting in the Dworkins' kitchen nook. Breakfast had been finished an hour ago. Jerry was noisily pulling a wooden train on wheels around the kitchen linoleum. Liberty appeared from nowhere and leaped into Emily's lap.

"Mother, I don't want to live in Connecticut. I might not even live in New York," Emily finally said.

A silence fell as Mrs. Crane regrouped. Marilyn poured more coffee.

Sid Hackett had dropped Emily off at the Dworkins' apartment late last night after she and Mike had returned to the city in an unmarked government car. Hackett had said she'd been brave. "But you're rash, Miss Crane," he'd added. "Courage and rashness can make for real trouble."

Marilyn passed Emily the sugar for her coffee. "Since you don't have a job that's worth anything—" Marilyn said.

"Yes, what *is* this job with that woman?" asked Mrs. Crane.

"She's very elderly, and I read to her," Emily said. That job was in another life. She felt drained.

"Well, the very idea!" said Mrs. Crane. "That you, with your college education, from Vassar no less, would even consider such a silly job. Honestly, Emily."

Emily resigned herself. Her mother would never admit that people could lose their jobs because of their politics and be forced to take jobs far below their training. But on this day, nothing Mrs. Crane said could really depress her. Her mother had been worried about her. Her mother had wept with worry.

"I'm all right now, Mother. Really." Emily stroked Liberty's back.

Mrs. Crane took a handkerchief out of her pocket and began dabbing at her eyes. "When I saw that apartment house with that big hole . . ."

Marilyn smiled. She knew that Emily had never felt her mother loved her. But now she knew differently. She reached her hand out for Emily's. "I'm sorry about Salwen. I didn't quite believe you."

"That's—understandable," Emily said. She smiled. "I know you didn't believe me."

"If you won't come back to Connecticut, where will you go?" asked Mrs. Crane.

"I don't know that I'll move anywhere, Mother. I won't spend the rest of my life with Miss Venable, though I'm really very fond of her. But I really want to get back to magazine work, to picture work." She was thinking of returning to the city with Mike. He'd kept his arm around her as they sat in the back of the car, their heads touching, all the way in.

"Do you think you can get hired?" Marilyn was asking. Jerry banged the train into the stove and was making a horrible exploding noise. "Jerry, stop that!"

"Yes," Emily said slowly, "I think I can. I think this whole terrible ordeal might just work out in my favor. I don't mean anyone's going to publicly admit anything but, anyway, yes, I think I can get a job." She smiled broadly.

Emily was coming down the street, headed for Miss Venable's house, when she saw him. Mike was leaning against the side of his car, his arms folded across his chest.

"Are you all right?" she asked.

"I'm fine. We had to wrap up the case. Took us till this morning," he said.

"What will happen to them?" she asked.

"They'll be extradited. I don't know where—a lot of countries want them—for all the reasons we know about."

"Are you sure?" she asked. "I mean, what's to

prevent the Defense Department from just quietly keeping them?"

"Nah," he said. "I called a friend at the *Times*. Story's out." He looked at her tenderly.

"I guess we did something, didn't we?" she said, walking over to him. "The two of us together."

"We stopped them," Cochran said, with a grin.

"You're a rare bird, Cochran."

"I never met anyone like you, either." He wanted to hold her close to him in the worst way. It was an ache he knew he would always feel next to his bones.

She had a lot to say to him but all the words were stopped up with emotion. "I waited for you."

"I guess I could have called," he replied. "I'm being transferred."

"Where?" The instant sadness caught her by surprise.

"Butte, Montana," Cochran said.

"I guess that isn't—the best spot for an FBI agent." When would she see him again? She knew it was her choice.

"Listen, I'm lucky I wasn't canned. And you know me, I don't like big cities anyway . . . like you do," he said. "I'll call you from Butte."

"I'd like that," she said.

"Safer, anyway," Cochran said.

They smiled at each other across their separate lives.

"You know, it wouldn't have worked," she said.

"I guess not," Cochran said.

"Too many things we don't believe the same," she said.

"Oil and water," Cochran said.

"Opposite sides," she said.

"You're right." He unlaced his arms and straightened up.

"Take care of yourself, Cochran." *I hope you call,* she thought. *I need to know where you are.*

"You, too, Emily," he said. He reached out his arm and she flowed into it in one smooth movement. They kissed, lightly at first, then more passionately with raw, eager youth. Gently, they disengaged.

She took a long look at him. "You have such great eyes," she said. She saw the open sky in his eyes. She turned toward Miss Venable's steps.

"Miss Crane?" Emily turned around. "We'd still like to talk to you," Cochran said, trying to laugh.

"I have nothing to say," she said. She put her nose in the air the way she had when they'd first met. "Yet," she added, flashing her finest smile. She went into the house, feeling him standing behind her. The door closed.